PAULINA
is generous and optimistic. She likes traveling and meeting people from all over the world.

Violet
is gentle and shy. Because of this, she can be taken to be a bit of a snobby rodent.

PHILIP SEYMOUR and **JONATHAN RHYMES**, famous writers for the prolific series of stories called THE ISLAND OF MYSTERY, attended MOUSEFORD ACADEMY. In their day, they loved their school and WHALE ISLAND and decided to add one more mystery to the island school!

Thea Stilton

PAPERCUTZ™

Thea Stilton

THE THEA SISTERS AND THE SECRET TREASURE HUNT

by Thea Stilton

PAPERCUT**Z**™

New York

THEA STILTON #8
"THE THEA SISTERS AND THE SECRET TREASURE HUNT"
Geronimo Stilton and Thea Stilton names, characters and related indicia are copyright,
trademark, and exclusive license of Atlantyca S.p.A.
All rights reserved.
The moral right of the author has been asserted.

Text by Thea Stilton
Cover by Ryan Jampole
Editorial supervision by Alessandra Berello and Chiara Richelmi (Atlantyca S.p.A.)
Script by Francesco Savino
Translation by Nanette McGuinness
Art by Ryan Jampole
Color by Laurie E. Smith
Lettering by Wilson Ramos Jr.

Based on an original idea by Elisabetta Dami

© Atlantyca S.p.A. – via Leopardi 8, 20123 Milano, Italia – foreignrights@atlantyca.it
© 2017 for this Work in English language by Papercutz, 160 Broadway, Suite 700, East
Wing, New York, NY 10038

www.geronimostilton.com

Stilton is a name of a famous English cheese. It is a registered trademark of the Stilton
Cheese Markers' Association.
For more information go to www.stiltoncheese.com

Production – Dawn Guzzo
Assistant Managing Editor – Jeff Whitman
Jim Salicrup
Editor-in-Chief

HC ISBN: 978-1-62991-836-5

Printed in China
December 2017

Papercutz books may be purchased for business or promotional use.
For information on bulk purchases, please contact Macmillan Corporate and Premium
Sales Department at (800) 221-7945 x5442.

Distributed by Macmillan
First Printing

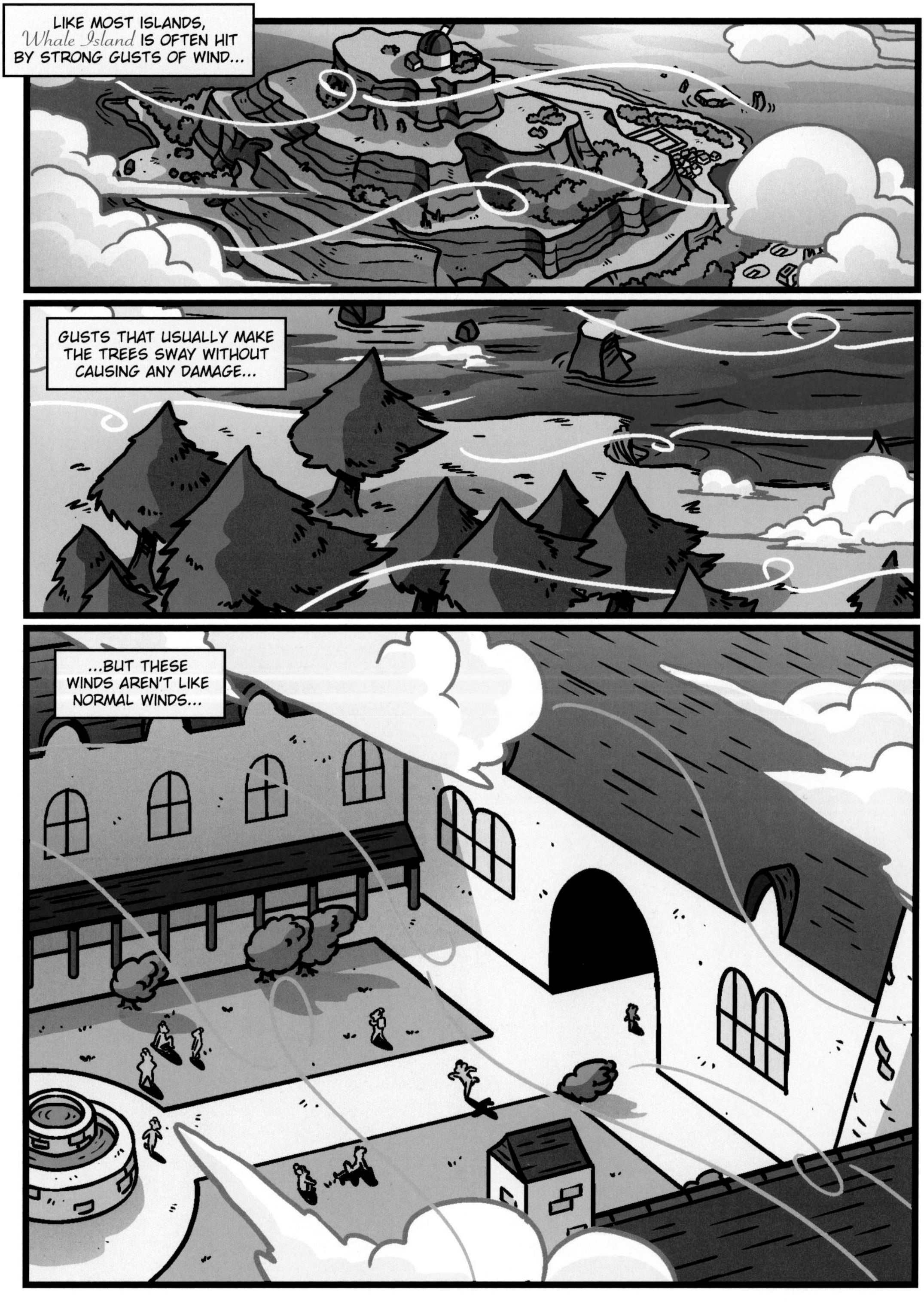
LIKE MOST ISLANDS, Whale Island IS OFTEN HIT BY STRONG GUSTS OF WIND...
GUSTS THAT USUALLY MAKE THE TREES SWAY WITHOUT CAUSING ANY DAMAGE...
...BUT THESE WINDS AREN'T LIKE NORMAL WINDS...

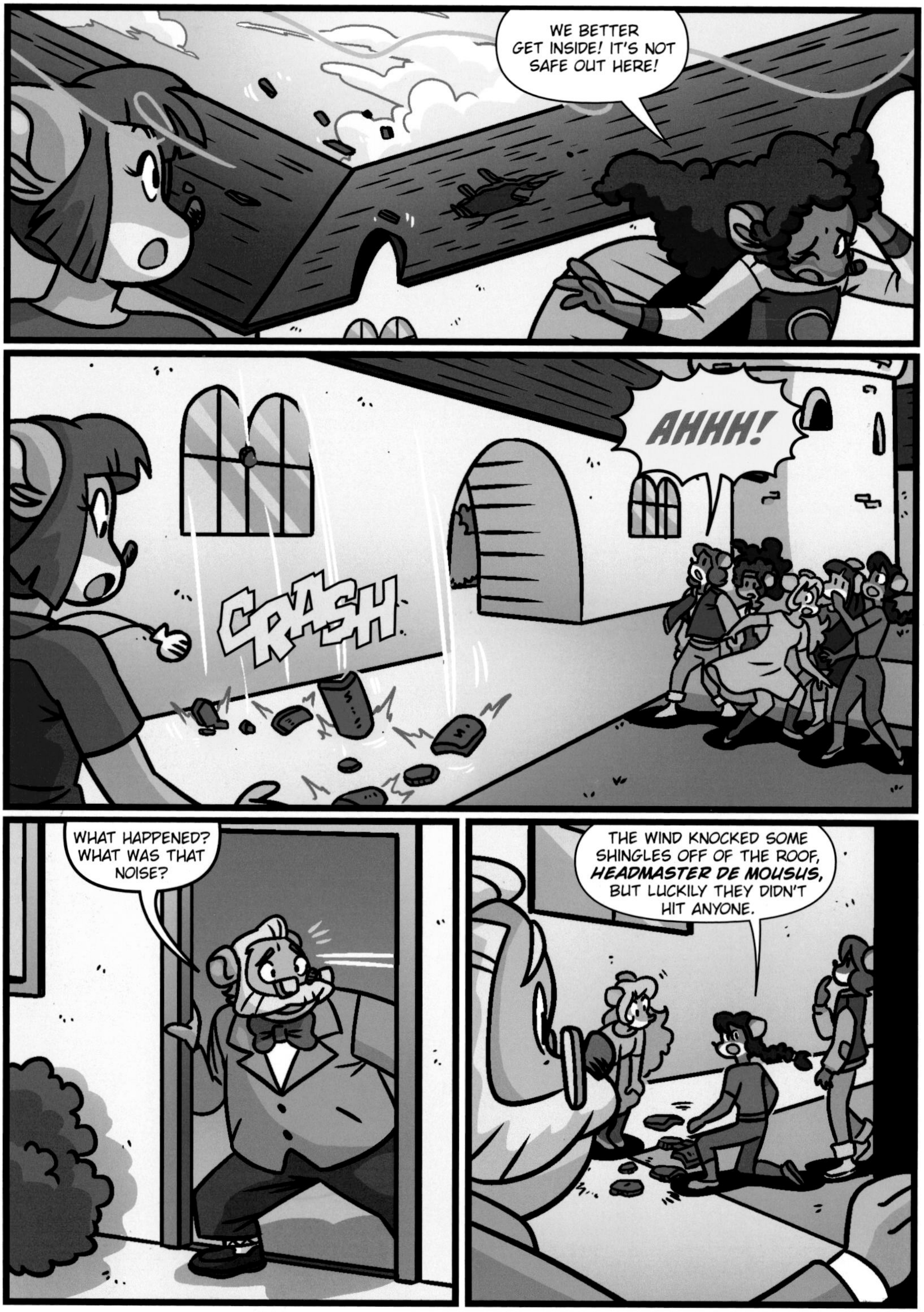
WE BETTER GET INSIDE! IT'S NOT SAFE OUT HERE!
AHHH!
CRASH
WHAT HAPPENED? WHAT WAS THAT NOISE?
THE WIND KNOCKED SOME SHINGLES OFF OF THE ROOF, ***HEADMASTER DE MOUSUS,*** BUT LUCKILY THEY DIDN'T HIT ANYONE.

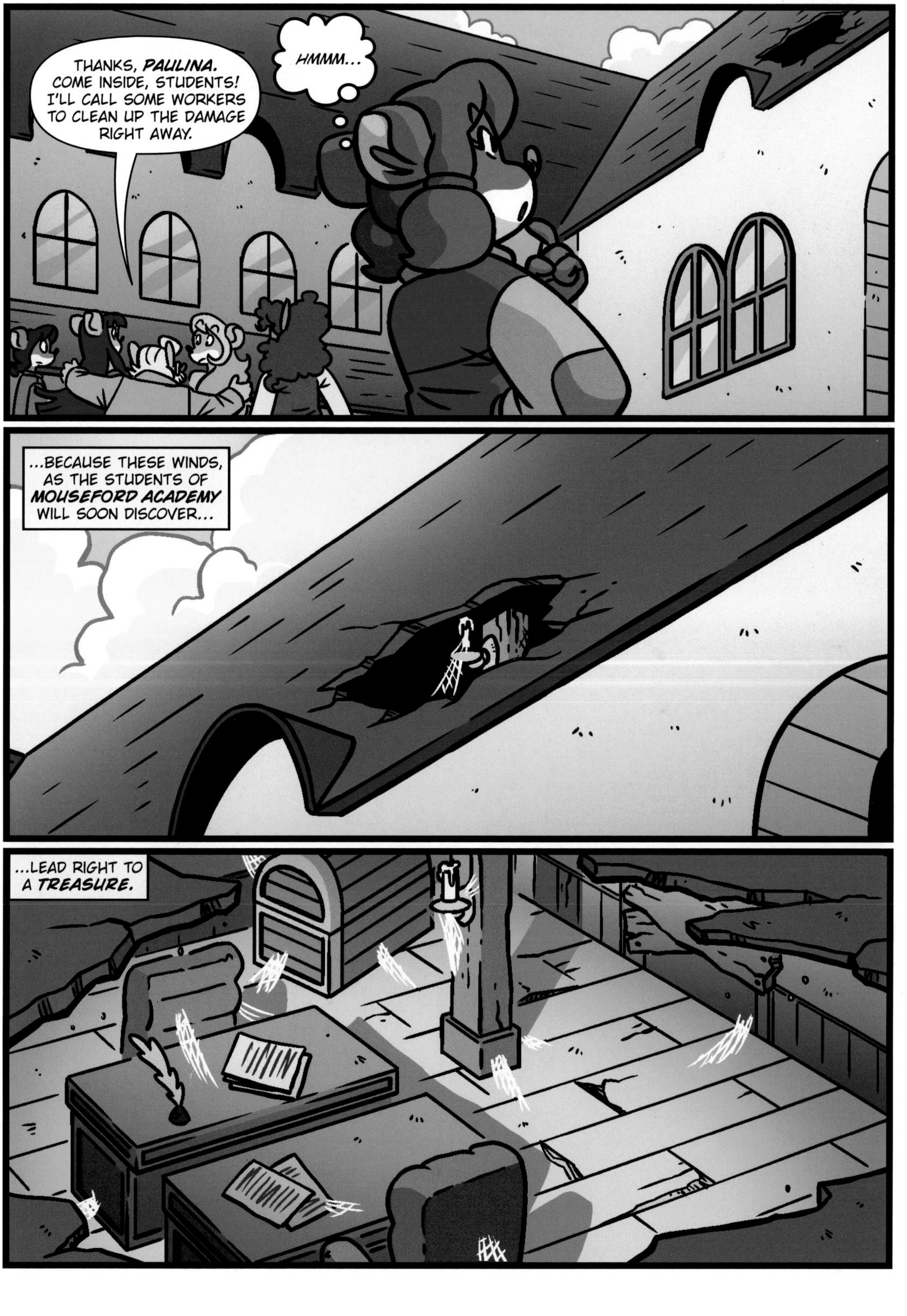
THANKS, PAULINA. COME INSIDE, STUDENTS! I'LL CALL SOME WORKERS TO CLEAN UP THE DAMAGE RIGHT AWAY.
HMMM...
...BECAUSE THESE WINDS, AS THE STUDENTS OF MOUSEFORD ACADEMY WILL SOON DISCOVER...
...LEAD RIGHT TO A TREASURE.

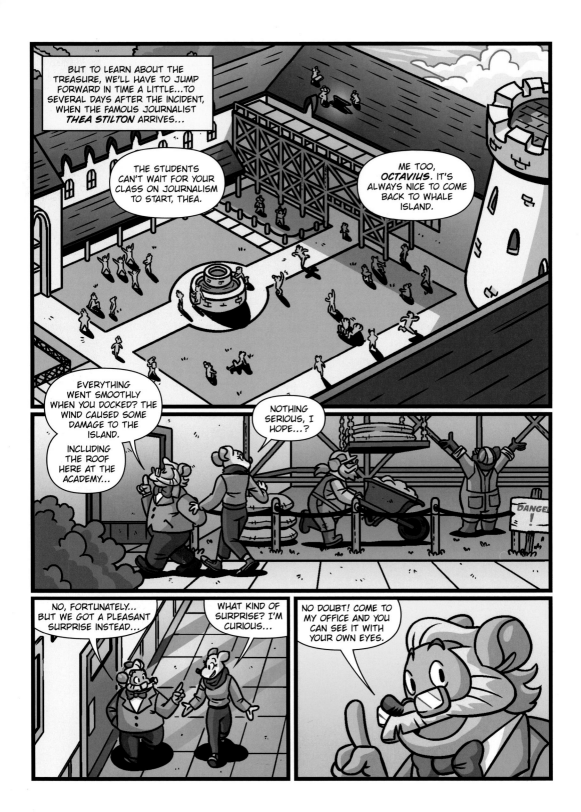

BUT TO LEARN ABOUT THE TREASURE, WE'LL HAVE TO JUMP FORWARD IN TIME A LITTLE...TO SEVERAL DAYS AFTER THE INCIDENT, WHEN THE FAMOUS JOURNALIST *THEA STILTON* ARRIVES...

THE STUDENTS CAN'T WAIT FOR YOUR CLASS ON JOURNALISM TO START, THEA.

ME TOO, *OCTAVIUS*. IT'S ALWAYS NICE TO COME BACK TO WHALE ISLAND.

EVERYTHING WENT SMOOTHLY WHEN YOU DOCKED? THE WIND CAUSED SOME DAMAGE TO THE ISLAND.

INCLUDING THE ROOF HERE AT THE ACADEMY...

NOTHING SERIOUS, I HOPE...?

DANGE !

NO, FORTUNATELY... BUT WE GOT A PLEASANT SURPRISE INSTEAD...

WHAT KIND OF SURPRISE? I'M CURIOUS...

NO DOUBT! COME TO MY OFFICE AND YOU CAN SEE IT WITH YOUR OWN EYES.

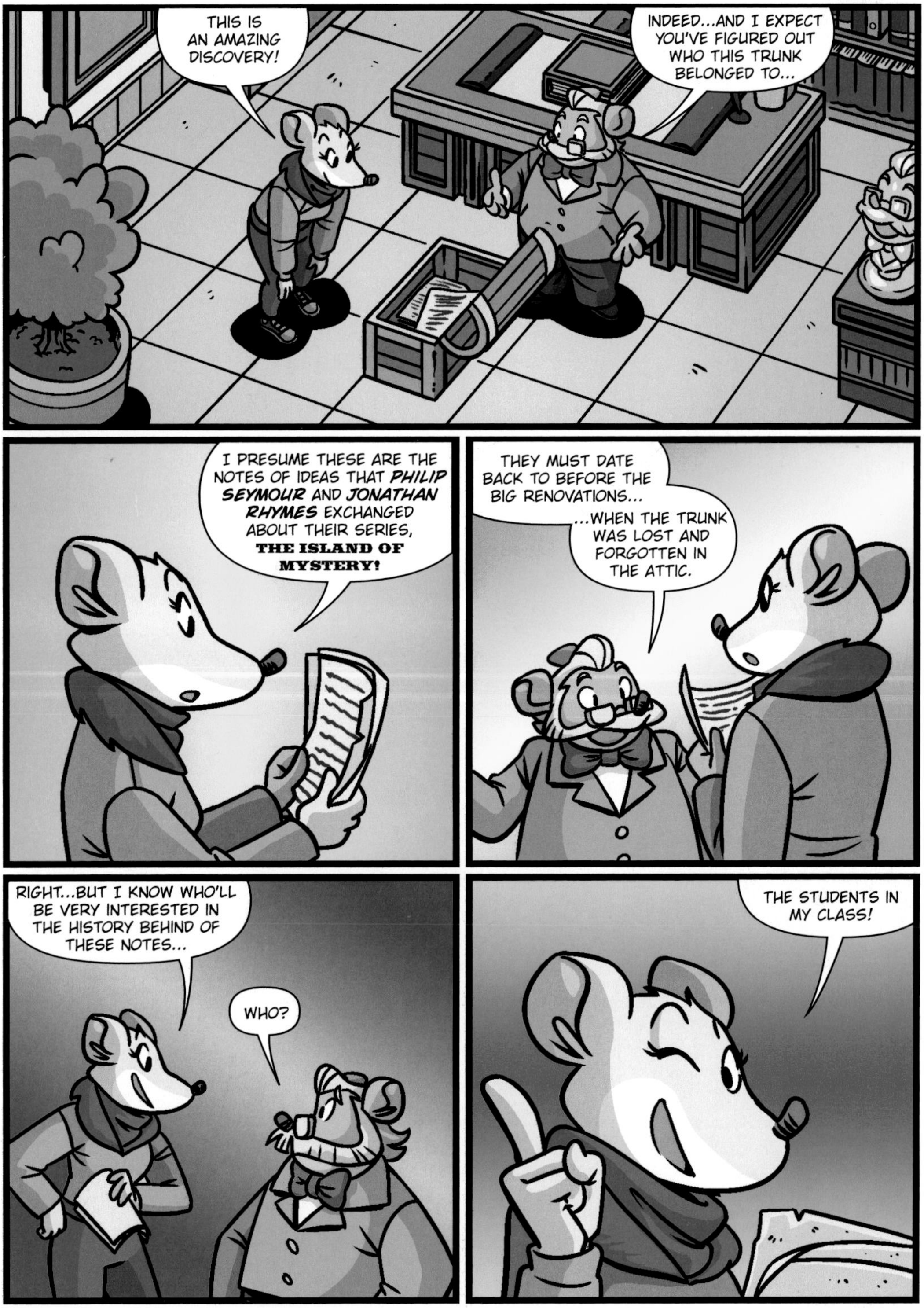
THIS IS AN AMAZING DISCOVERY!
INDEED...AND I EXPECT YOU'VE FIGURED OUT WHO THIS TRUNK BELONGED TO...
I PRESUME THESE ARE THE NOTES OF IDEAS THAT PHILIP SEYMOUR AND JONATHAN RHYMES EXCHANGED ABOUT THEIR SERIES, THE ISLAND OF MYSTERY!
THEY MUST DATE BACK TO BEFORE THE BIG RENOVATIONS...
...WHEN THE TRUNK WAS LOST AND FORGOTTEN IN THE ATTIC.
RIGHT...BUT I KNOW WHO'LL BE VERY INTERESTED IN THE HISTORY BEHIND OF THESE NOTES...
WHO?
THE STUDENTS IN MY CLASS!

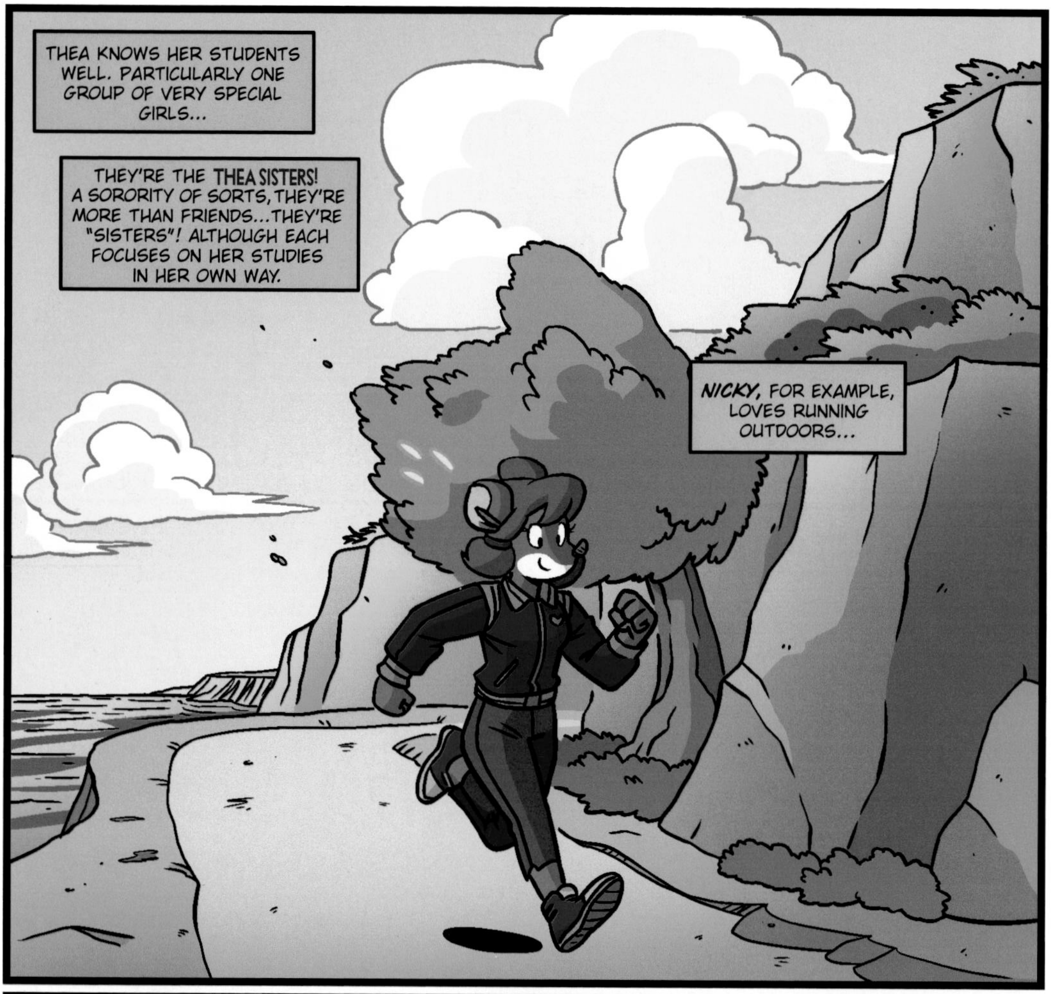
THEA KNOWS HER STUDENTS WELL. PARTICULARLY ONE GROUP OF VERY SPECIAL GIRLS...
THEY'RE THE THEA SISTERS! A SORORITY OF SORTS, THEY'RE MORE THAN FRIENDS...THEY'RE "SISTERS"! ALTHOUGH EACH FOCUSES ON HER STUDIES IN HER OWN WAY.
NICKY, FOR EXAMPLE, LOVES RUNNING OUTDOORS...

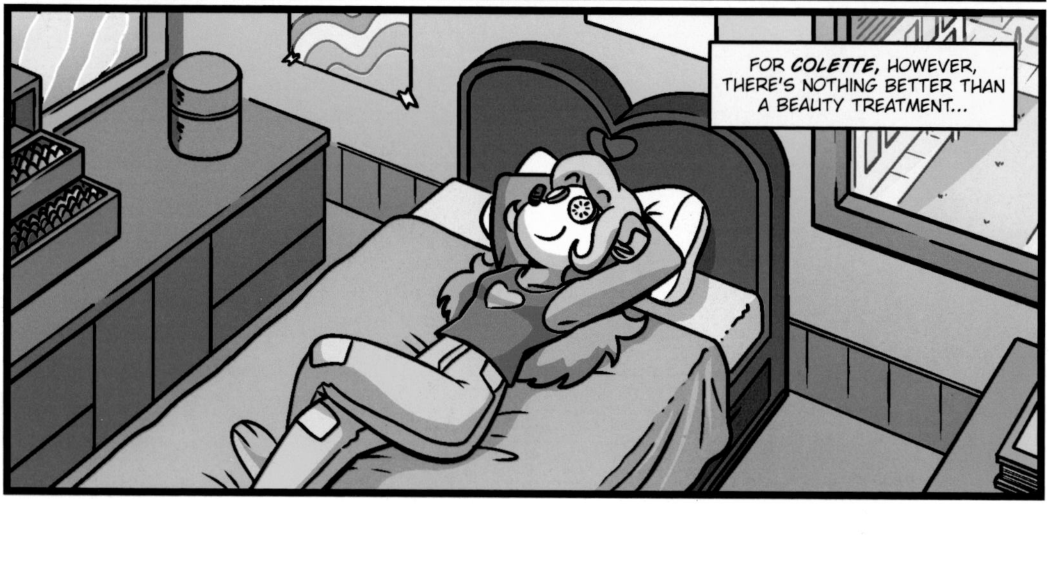
FOR COLETTE, HOWEVER, THERE'S NOTHING BETTER THAN A BEAUTY TREATMENT...

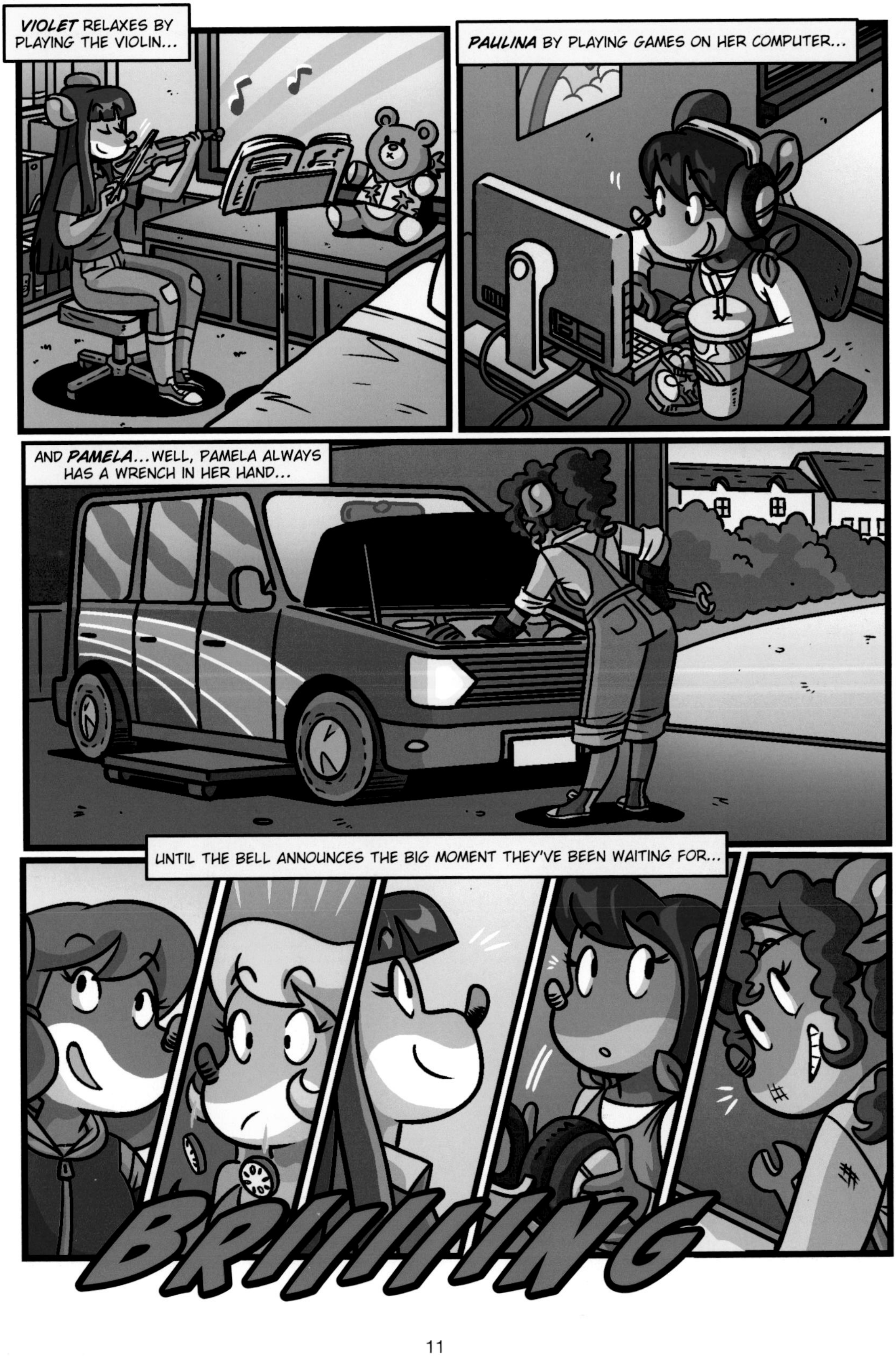
VIOLET RELAXES BY PLAYING THE VIOLIN...
PAULINA BY PLAYING GAMES ON HER COMPUTER...
AND PAMELA... WELL, PAMELA ALWAYS HAS A WRENCH IN HER HAND...
UNTIL THE BELL ANNOUNCES THE BIG MOMENT THEY'VE BEEN WAITING FOR...
BRIIIIING

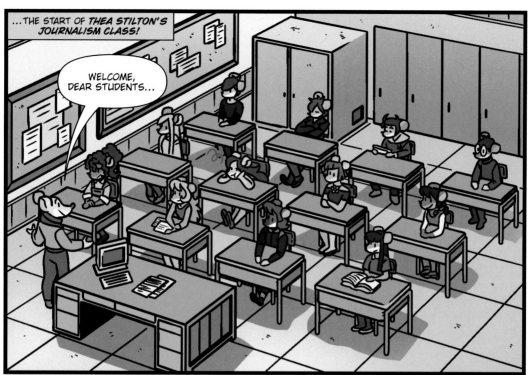

...THE START OF *THEA STILTON'S JOURNALISM CLASS!*

WELCOME, DEAR STUDENTS...

IT'S ALWAYS A PLEASURE TO BE HERE AT MOUSEFORD ACADEMY WITH YOU!

ZOE, I BET THIS WILL BE ANOTHER **BORING** CLASS!

THINK SO, *VANILLA?* HEE! HEE!

SHHH!

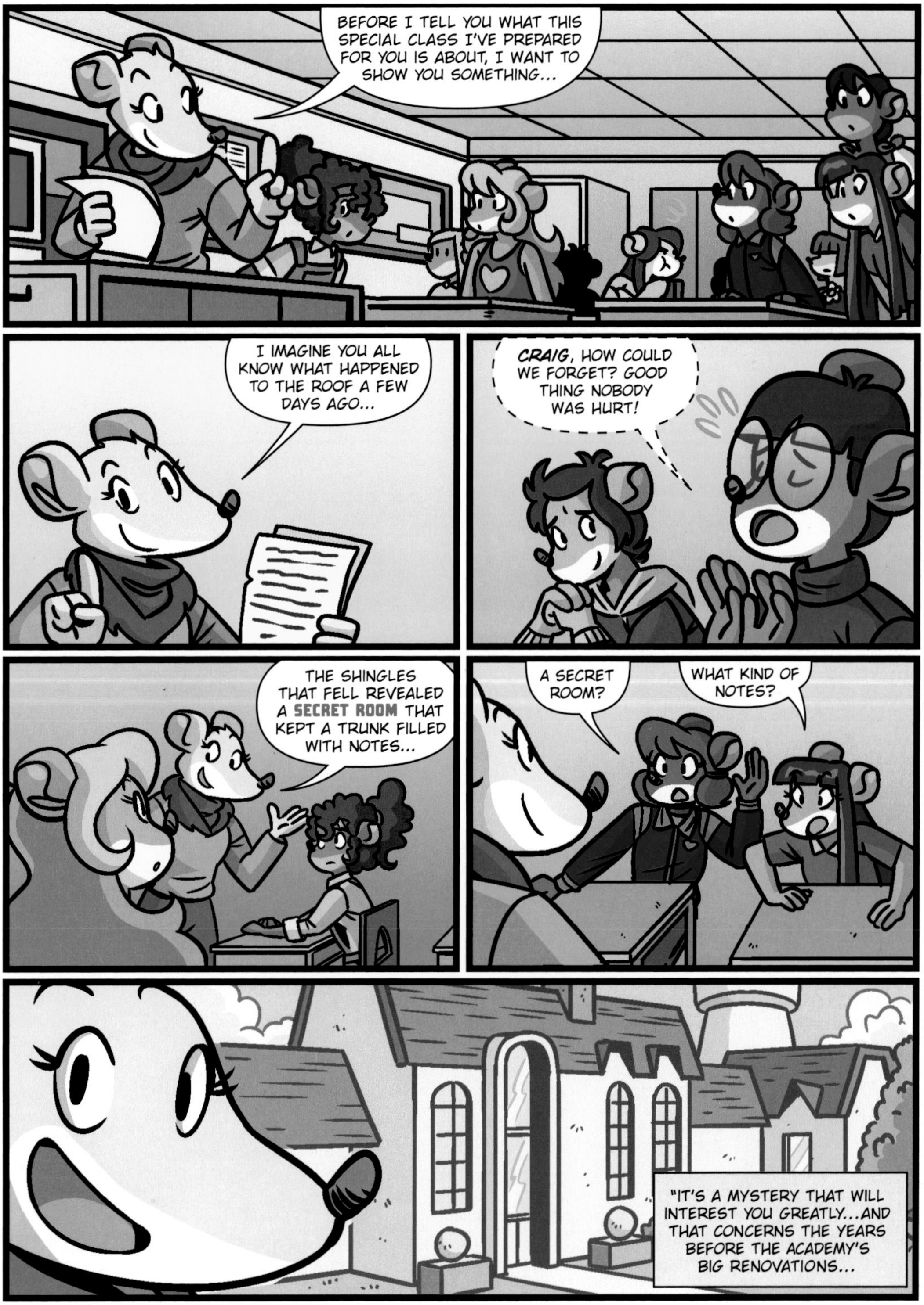

BEFORE I TELL YOU WHAT THIS SPECIAL CLASS I'VE PREPARED FOR YOU IS ABOUT, I WANT TO SHOW YOU SOMETHING...
I IMAGINE YOU ALL KNOW WHAT HAPPENED TO THE ROOF A FEW DAYS AGO...
CRAIG, HOW COULD WE FORGET? GOOD THING NOBODY WAS HURT!
THE SHINGLES THAT FELL REVEALED A SECRET ROOM THAT KEPT A TRUNK FILLED WITH NOTES...
A SECRET ROOM?
WHAT KIND OF NOTES?
"IT'S A MYSTERY THAT WILL INTEREST YOU GREATLY...AND THAT CONCERNS THE YEARS BEFORE THE ACADEMY'S BIG RENOVATIONS...

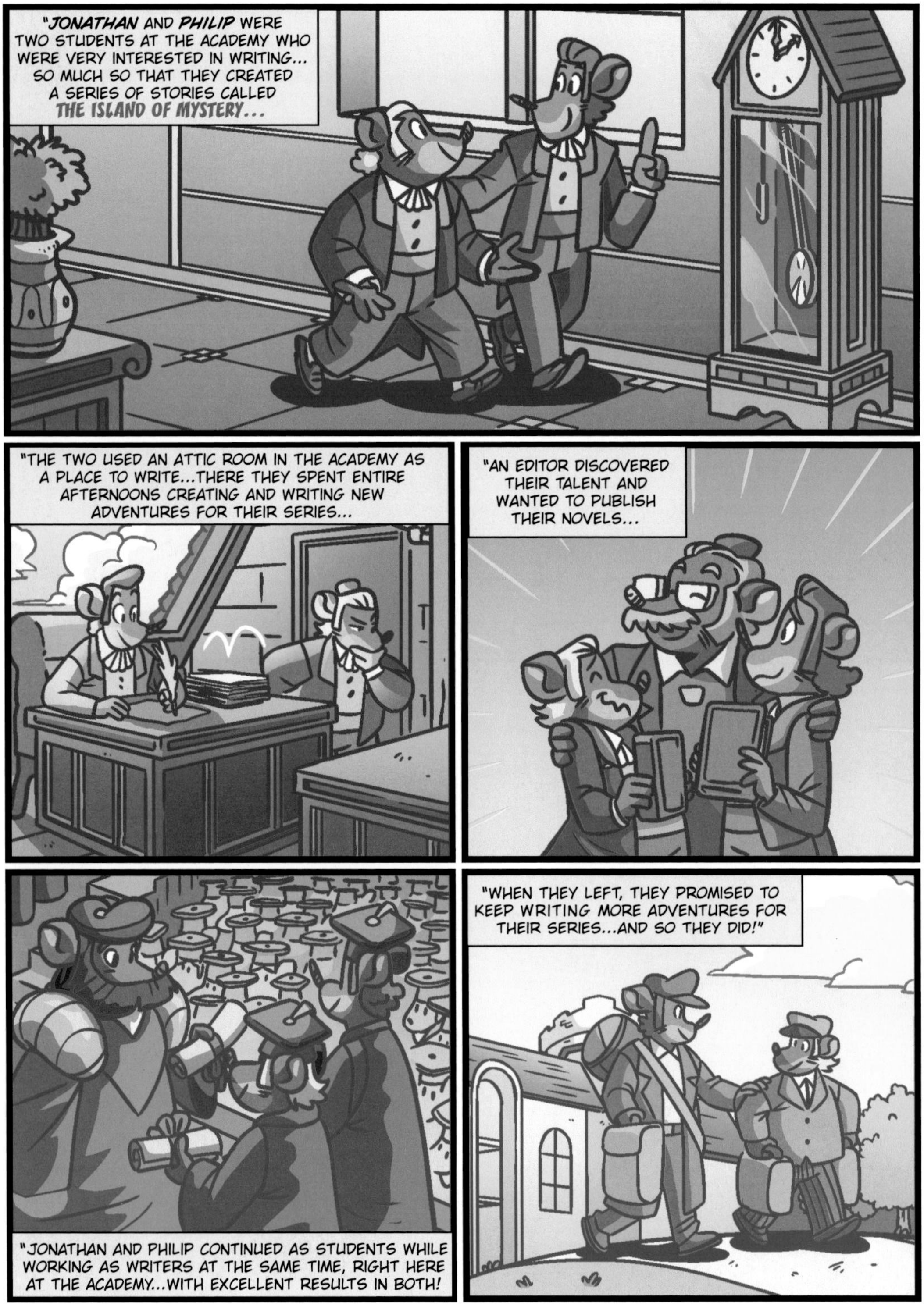
"JONATHAN AND PHILIP WERE TWO STUDENTS AT THE ACADEMY WHO WERE VERY INTERESTED IN WRITING... SO MUCH SO THAT THEY CREATED A SERIES OF STORIES CALLED THE ISLAND OF MYSTERY...
"THE TWO USED AN ATTIC ROOM IN THE ACADEMY AS A PLACE TO WRITE...THERE THEY SPENT ENTIRE AFTERNOONS CREATING AND WRITING NEW ADVENTURES FOR THEIR SERIES...
"AN EDITOR DISCOVERED THEIR TALENT AND WANTED TO PUBLISH THEIR NOVELS...
"JONATHAN AND PHILIP CONTINUED AS STUDENTS WHILE WORKING AS WRITERS AT THE SAME TIME, RIGHT HERE AT THE ACADEMY...WITH EXCELLENT RESULTS IN BOTH!
"WHEN THEY LEFT, THEY PROMISED TO KEEP WRITING MORE ADVENTURES FOR THEIR SERIES...AND SO THEY DID!"

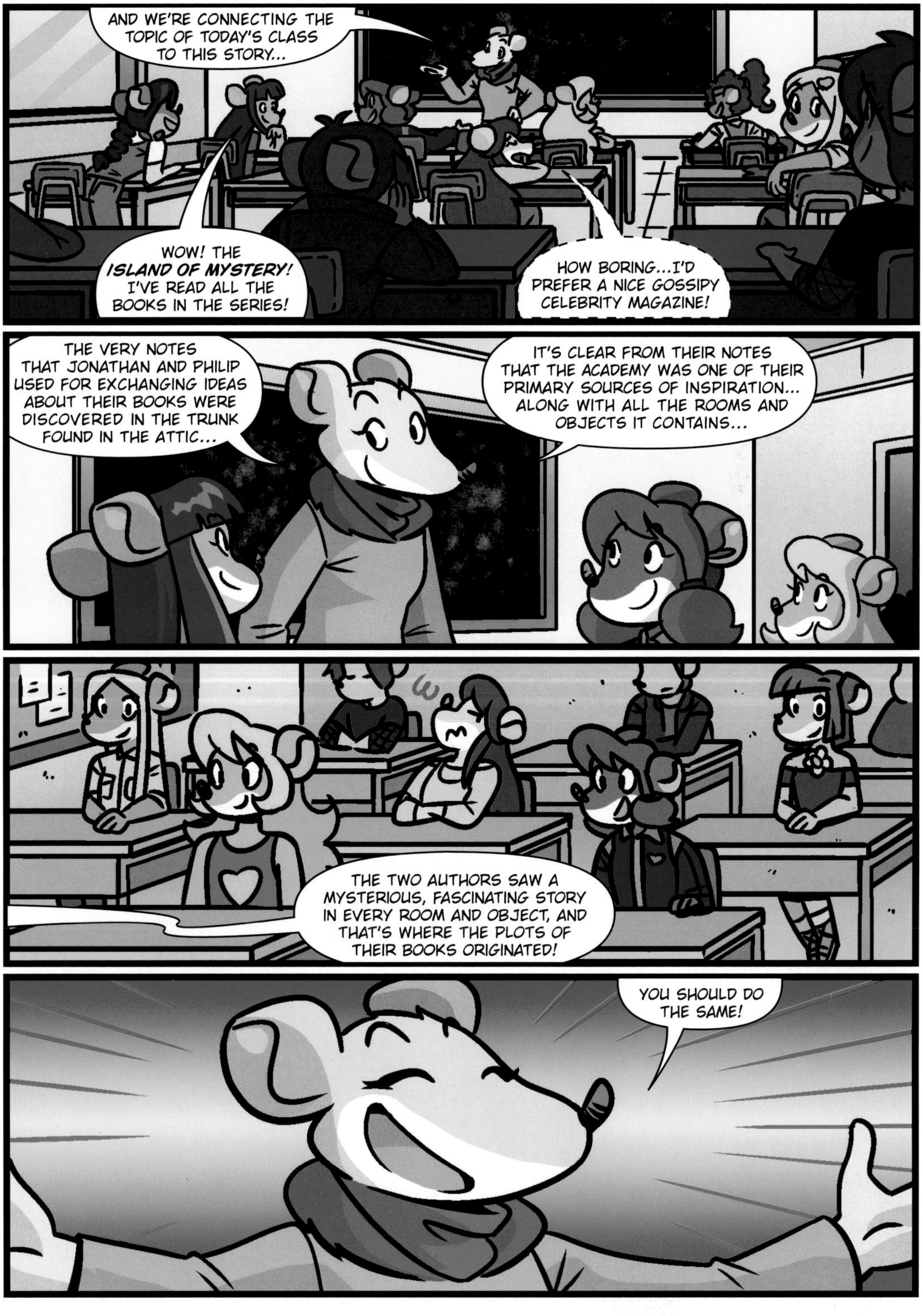
AND WE'RE CONNECTING THE TOPIC OF TODAY'S CLASS TO THIS STORY...
WOW! THE *ISLAND OF MYSTERY!* I'VE READ ALL THE BOOKS IN THE SERIES!
HOW BORING...I'D PREFER A NICE GOSSIPY CELEBRITY MAGAZINE!
THE VERY NOTES THAT JONATHAN AND PHILIP USED FOR EXCHANGING IDEAS ABOUT THEIR BOOKS WERE DISCOVERED IN THE TRUNK FOUND IN THE ATTIC...
IT'S CLEAR FROM THEIR NOTES THAT THE ACADEMY WAS ONE OF THEIR PRIMARY SOURCES OF INSPIRATION... ALONG WITH ALL THE ROOMS AND OBJECTS IT CONTAINS...
THE TWO AUTHORS SAW A MYSTERIOUS, FASCINATING STORY IN EVERY ROOM AND OBJECT, AND THAT'S WHERE THE PLOTS OF THEIR BOOKS ORIGINATED!
YOU SHOULD DO THE SAME!

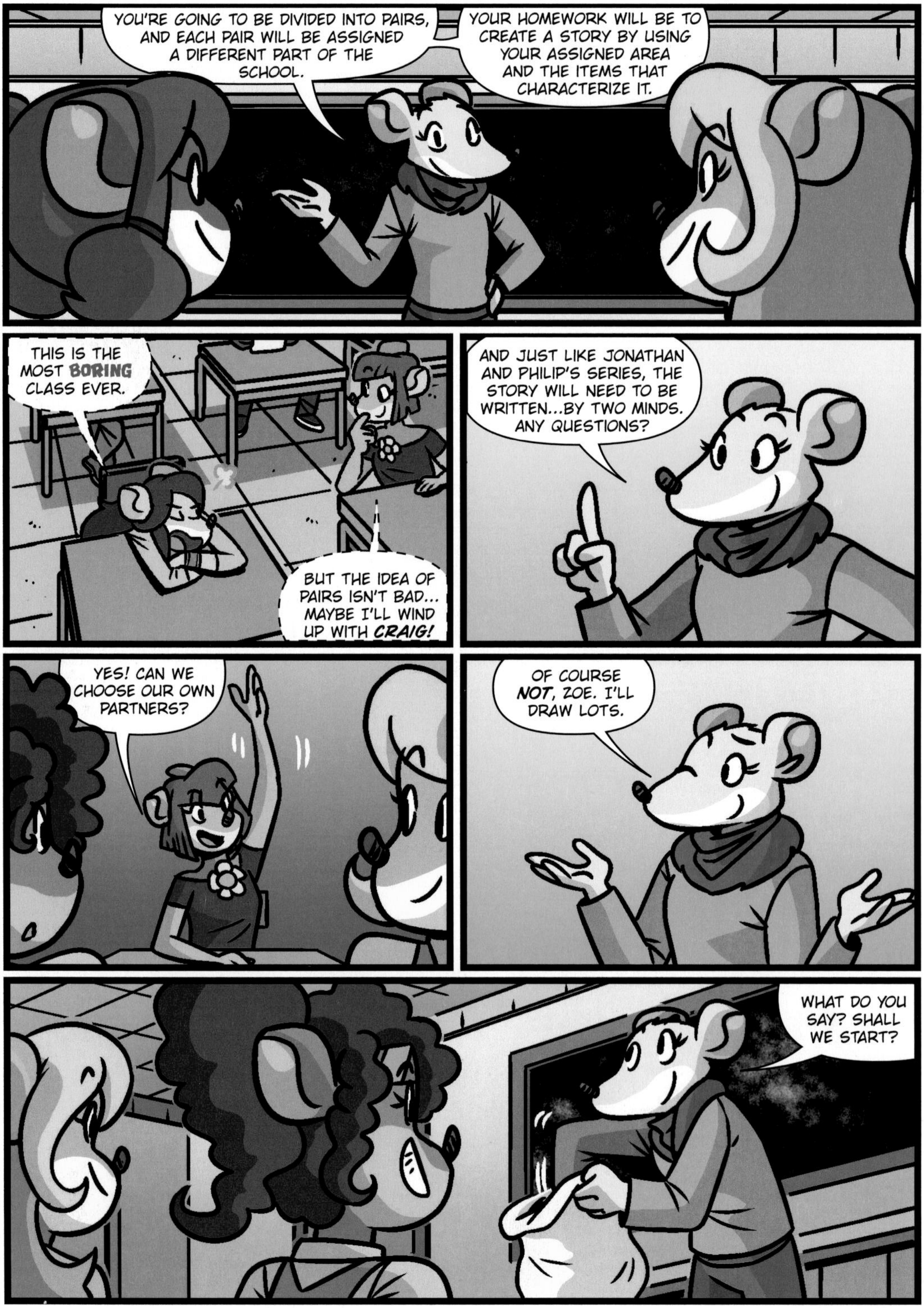
YOU'RE GOING TO BE DIVIDED INTO PAIRS, AND EACH PAIR WILL BE ASSIGNED A DIFFERENT PART OF THE SCHOOL.
YOUR HOMEWORK WILL BE TO CREATE A STORY BY USING YOUR ASSIGNED AREA AND THE ITEMS THAT CHARACTERIZE IT.
THIS IS THE MOST BORING CLASS EVER.
BUT THE IDEA OF PAIRS ISN'T BAD... MAYBE I'LL WIND UP WITH CRAIG!
AND JUST LIKE JONATHAN AND PHILIP'S SERIES, THE STORY WILL NEED TO BE WRITTEN...BY TWO MINDS. ANY QUESTIONS?
YES! CAN WE CHOOSE OUR OWN PARTNERS?
OF COURSE NOT, ZOE. I'LL DRAW LOTS.
WHAT DO YOU SAY? SHALL WE START?

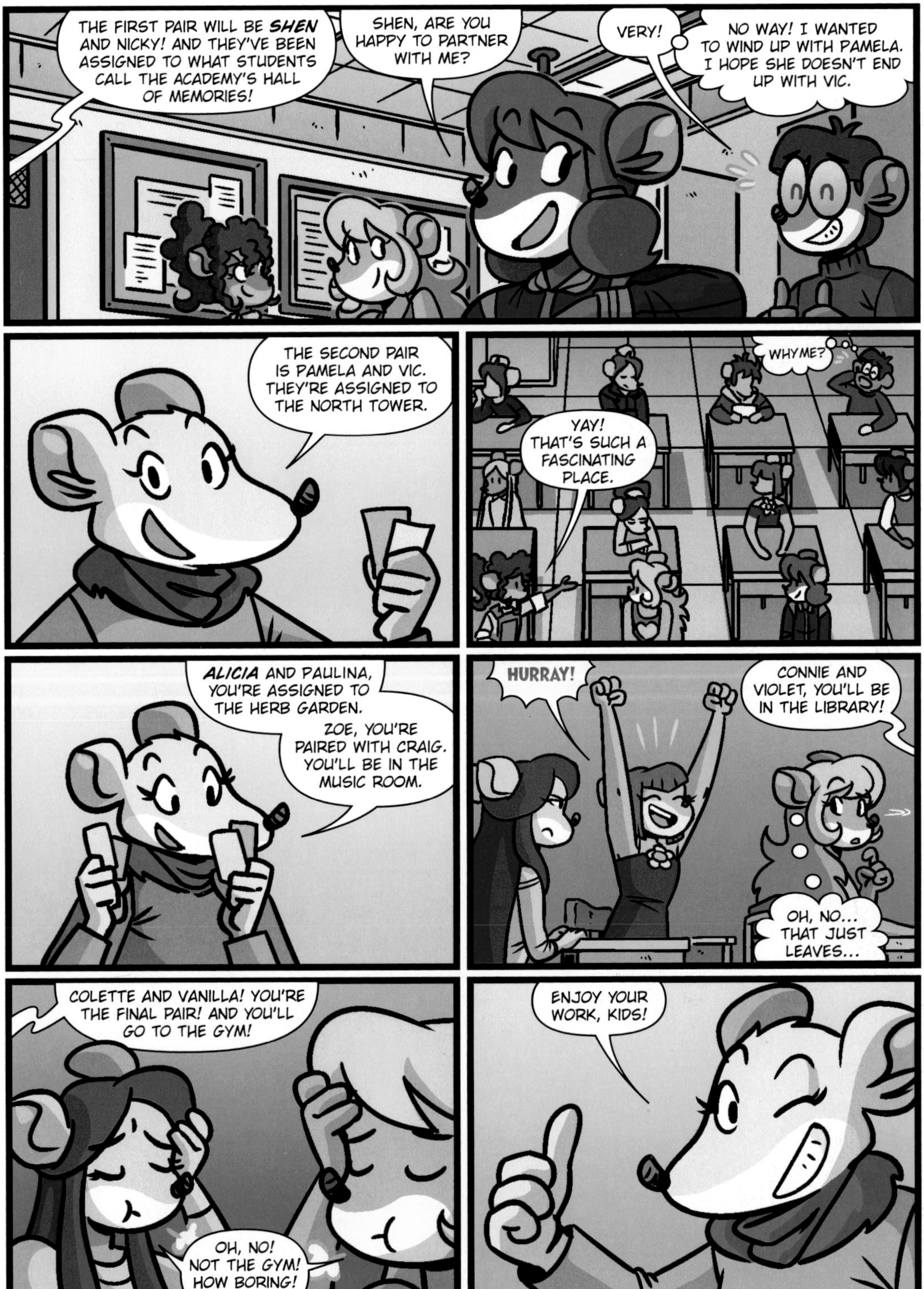
THE FIRST PAIR WILL BE SHEN AND NICKY! AND THEY'VE BEEN ASSIGNED TO WHAT STUDENTS CALL THE ACADEMY'S HALL OF MEMORIES!
SHEN, ARE YOU HAPPY TO PARTNER WITH ME?
VERY!
NO WAY! I WANTED TO WIND UP WITH PAMELA. I HOPE SHE DOESN'T END UP WITH VIC.
THE SECOND PAIR IS PAMELA AND VIC. THEY'RE ASSIGNED TO THE NORTH TOWER.
WHY ME?
YAY! THAT'S SUCH A FASCINATING PLACE.
ALICIA AND PAULINA, YOU'RE ASSIGNED TO THE HERB GARDEN.
ZOE, YOU'RE PAIRED WITH CRAIG. YOU'LL BE IN THE MUSIC ROOM.
HURRAY!
CONNIE AND VIOLET, YOU'LL BE IN THE LIBRARY!
OH, NO... THAT JUST LEAVES...
COLETTE AND VANILLA! YOU'RE THE FINAL PAIR! AND YOU'LL GO TO THE GYM!
OH, NO! NOT THE GYM! HOW BORING!
ENJOY YOUR WORK, KIDS!

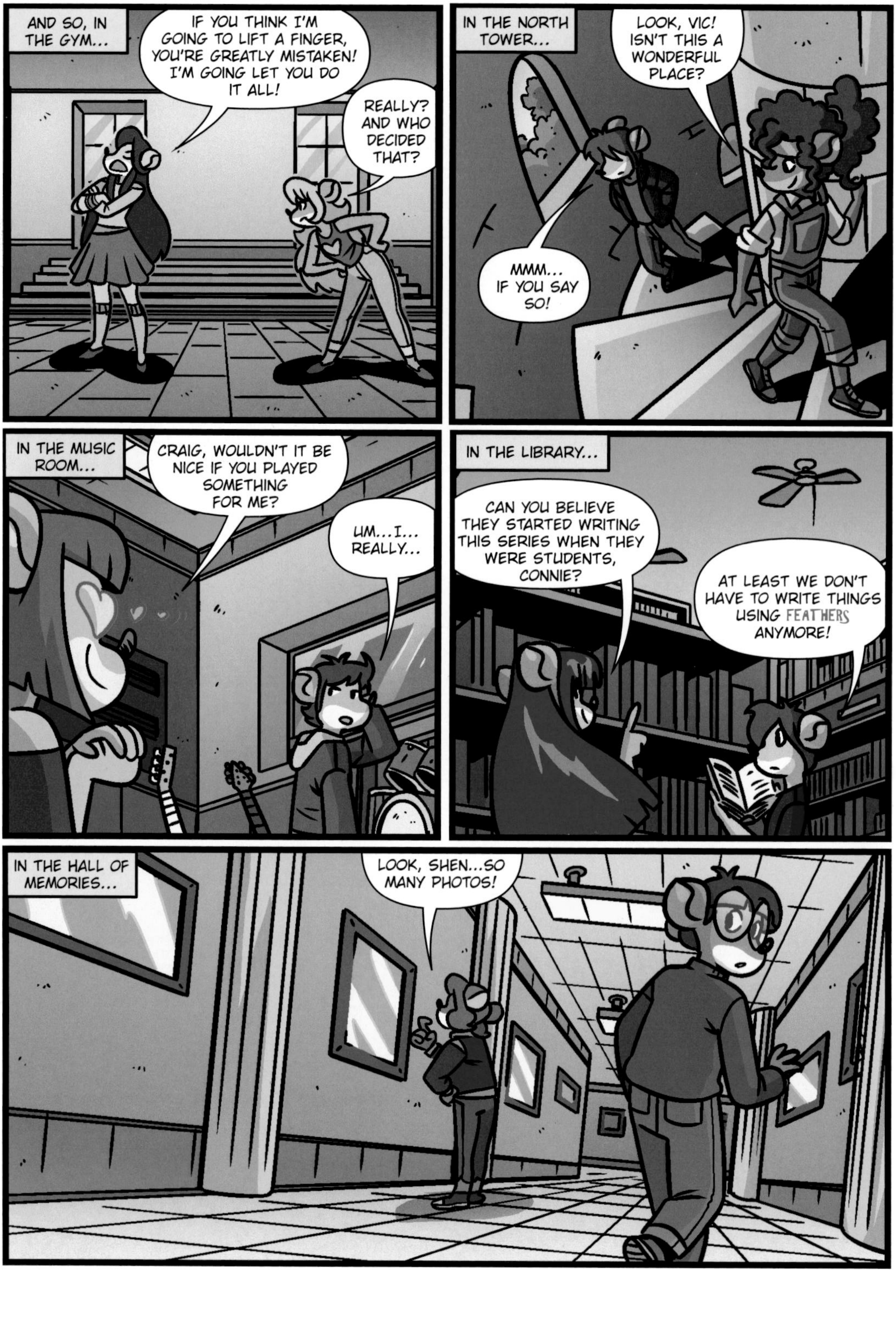
AND SO, IN THE GYM...
IF YOU THINK I'M GOING TO LIFT A FINGER, YOU'RE GREATLY MISTAKEN! I'M GOING LET YOU DO IT ALL!
REALLY? AND WHO DECIDED THAT?
IN THE NORTH TOWER...
LOOK, VIC! ISN'T THIS A WONDERFUL PLACE?
MMM... IF YOU SAY SO!
IN THE MUSIC ROOM...
CRAIG, WOULDN'T IT BE NICE IF YOU PLAYED SOMETHING FOR ME?
UM...I... REALLY...
IN THE LIBRARY...
CAN YOU BELIEVE THEY STARTED WRITING THIS SERIES WHEN THEY WERE STUDENTS, CONNIE?
AT LEAST WE DON'T HAVE TO WRITE THINGS USING FEATHERS ANYMORE!
IN THE HALL OF MEMORIES...
LOOK, SHEN...SO MANY PHOTOS!

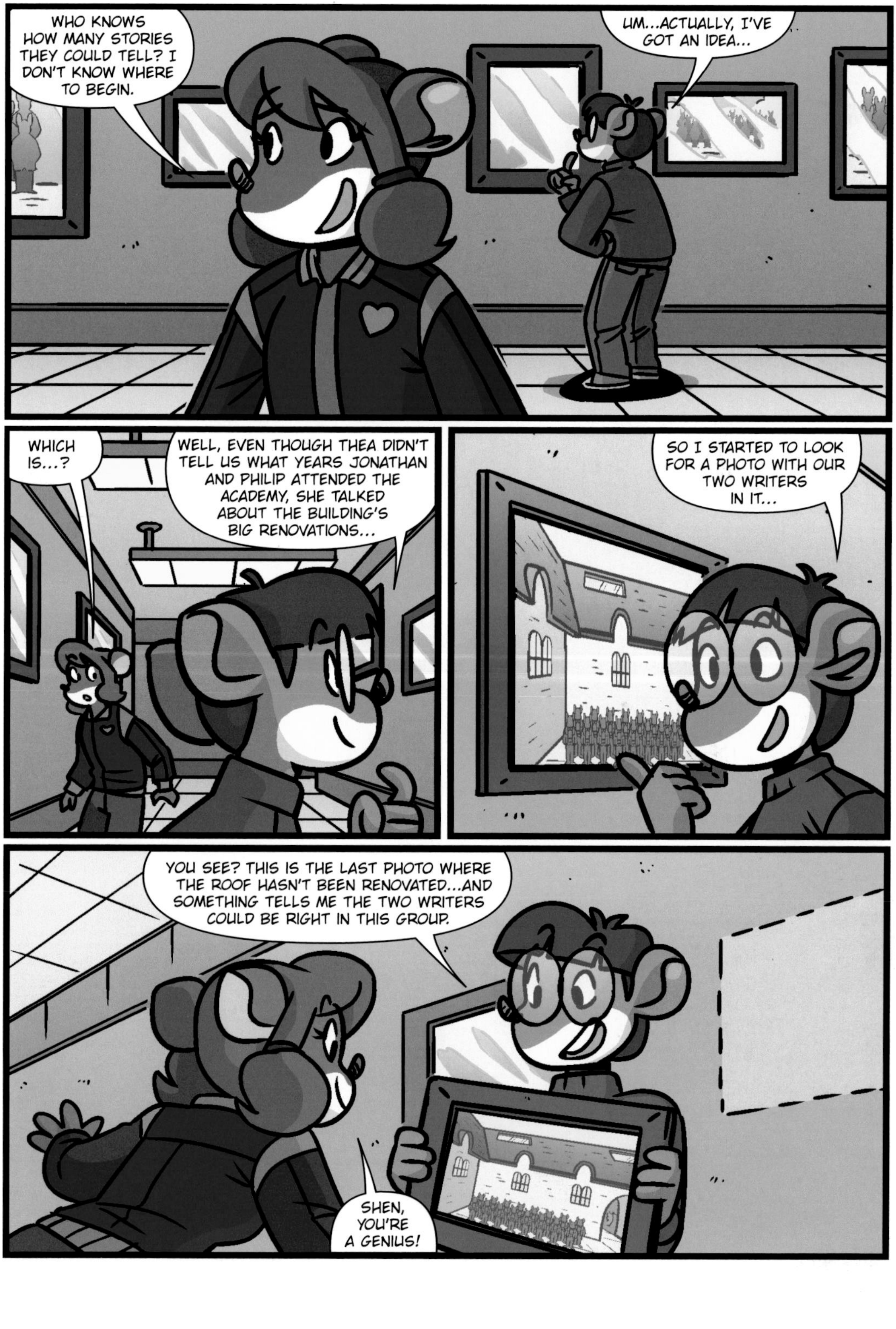
WHO KNOWS HOW MANY STORIES THEY COULD TELL? I DON'T KNOW WHERE TO BEGIN.
UM...ACTUALLY, I'VE GOT AN IDEA...
WHICH IS...?
WELL, EVEN THOUGH THEA DIDN'T TELL US WHAT YEARS JONATHAN AND PHILIP ATTENDED THE ACADEMY, SHE TALKED ABOUT THE BUILDING'S BIG RENOVATIONS...
SO I STARTED TO LOOK FOR A PHOTO WITH OUR TWO WRITERS IN IT...
YOU SEE? THIS IS THE LAST PHOTO WHERE THE ROOF HASN'T BEEN RENOVATED...AND SOMETHING TELLS ME THE TWO WRITERS COULD BE RIGHT IN THIS GROUP.
SHEN, YOU'RE A GENIUS!

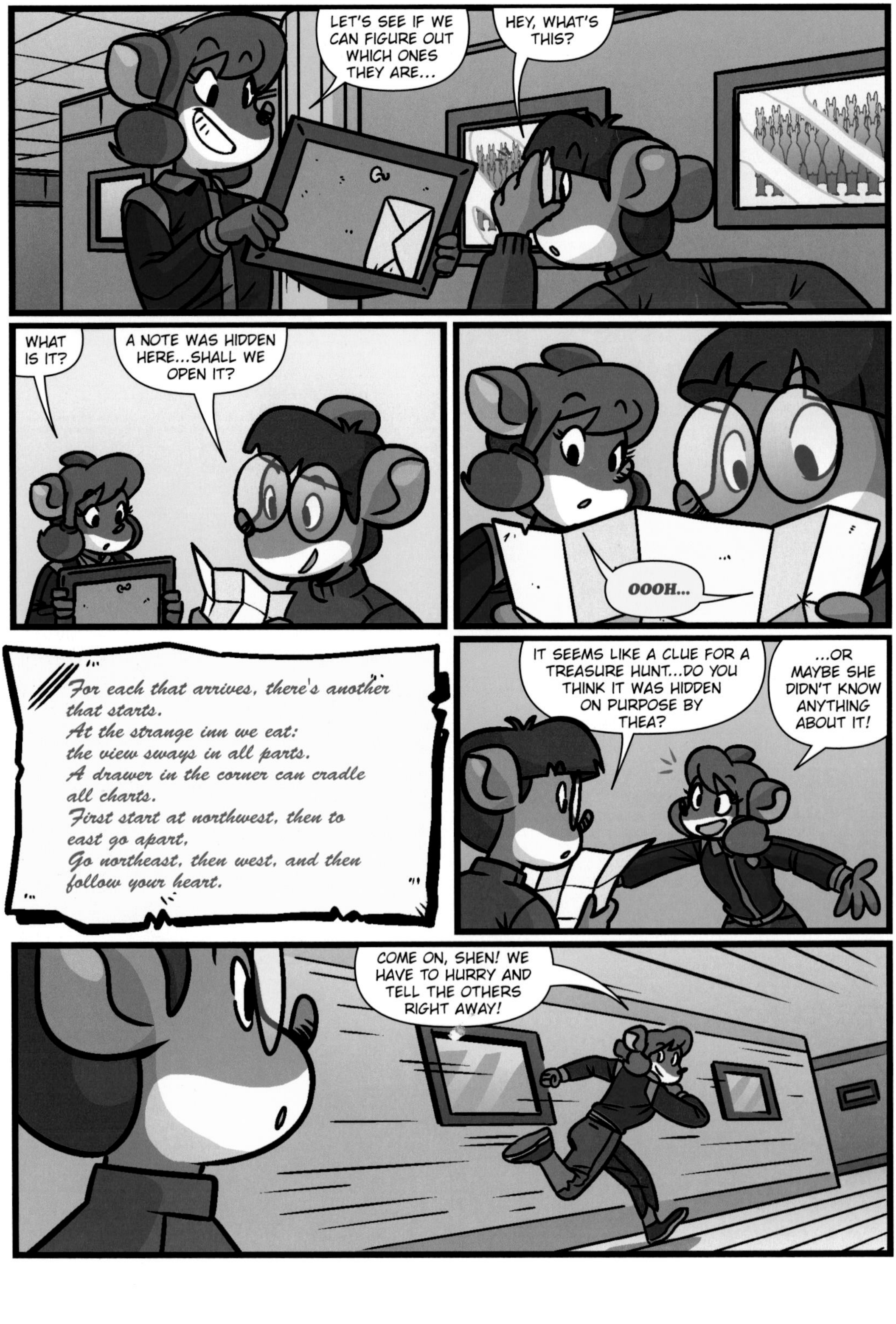
LET'S SEE IF WE CAN FIGURE OUT WHICH ONES THEY ARE...
HEY, WHAT'S THIS?
WHAT IS IT?
A NOTE WAS HIDDEN HERE...SHALL WE OPEN IT?
OOOH...
For each that arrives, there's another that starts.
At the strange inn we eat:
the view sways in all parts.
A drawer in the corner can cradle all charts.
First start at northwest, then to east go apart,
Go northeast, then west, and then follow your heart.
IT SEEMS LIKE A CLUE FOR A TREASURE HUNT...DO YOU THINK IT WAS HIDDEN ON PURPOSE BY THEA?
...OR MAYBE SHE DIDN'T KNOW ANYTHING ABOUT IT!
COME ON, SHEN! WE HAVE TO HURRY AND TELL THE OTHERS RIGHT AWAY!

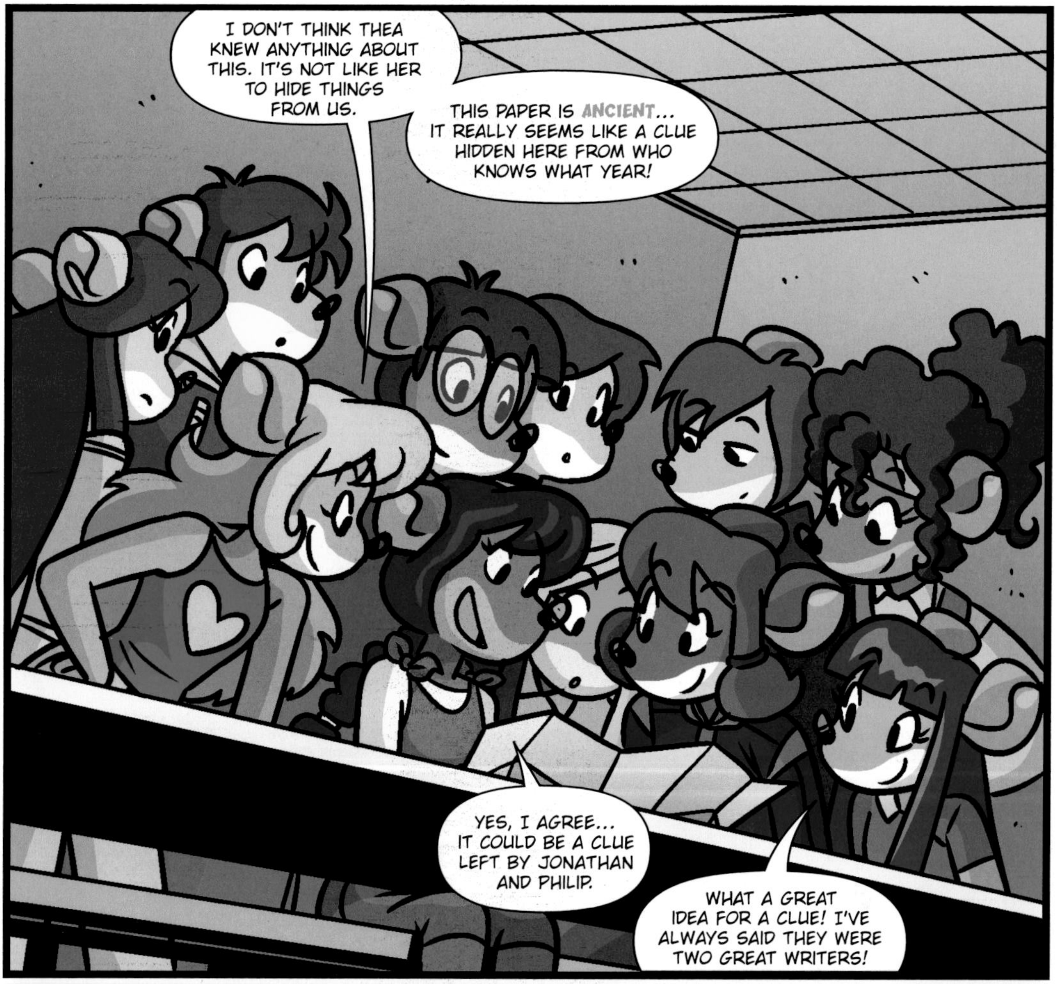
I DON'T THINK THEA KNEW ANYTHING ABOUT THIS. IT'S NOT LIKE HER TO HIDE THINGS FROM US.
THIS PAPER IS ANCIENT... IT REALLY SEEMS LIKE A CLUE HIDDEN HERE FROM WHO KNOWS WHAT YEAR!
YES, I AGREE... IT COULD BE A CLUE LEFT BY JONATHAN AND PHILIP.
WHAT A GREAT IDEA FOR A CLUE! I'VE ALWAYS SAID THEY WERE TWO GREAT WRITERS!

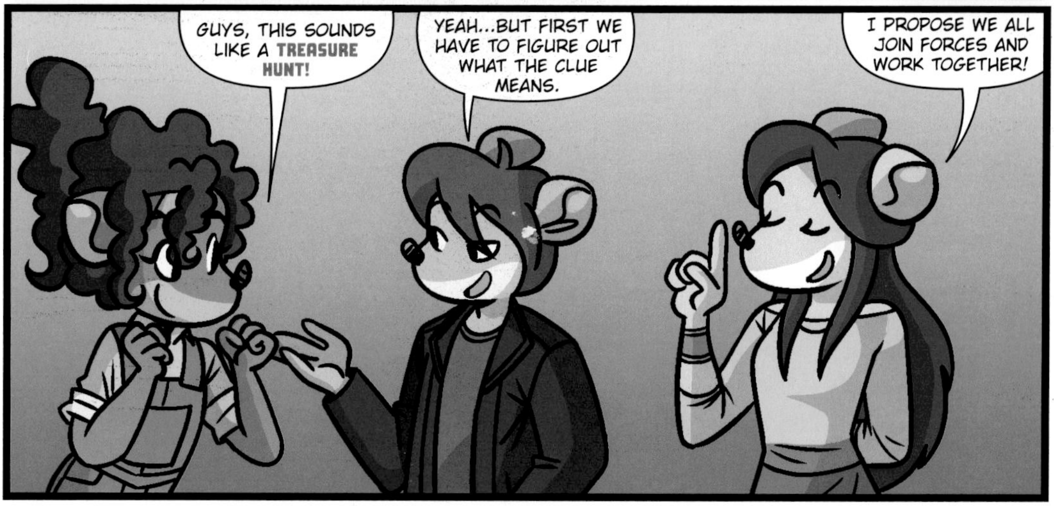
GUYS, THIS SOUNDS LIKE A TREASURE HUNT!
YEAH...BUT FIRST WE HAVE TO FIGURE OUT WHAT THE CLUE MEANS.
I PROPOSE WE ALL JOIN FORCES AND WORK TOGETHER!

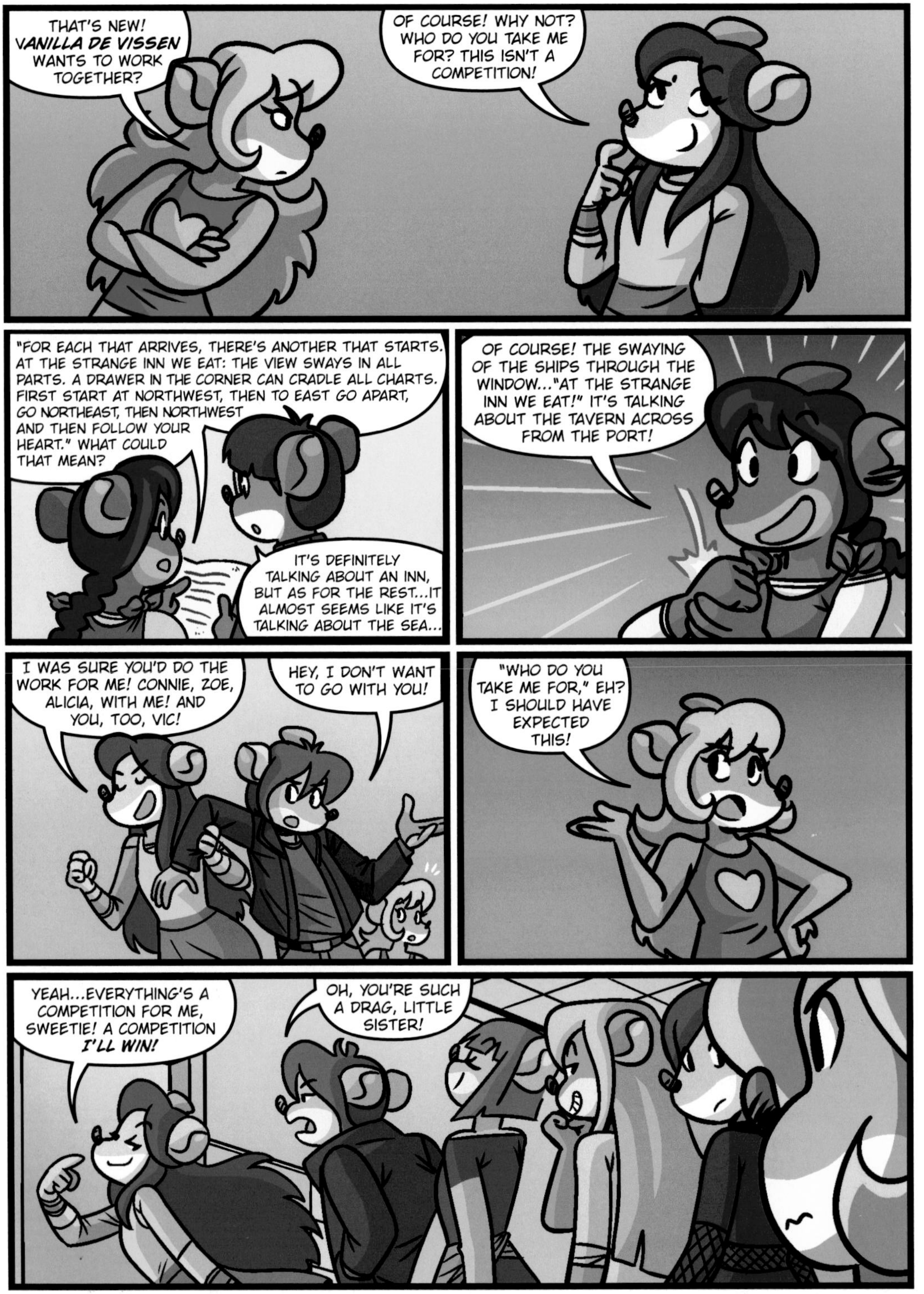
THAT'S NEW! VANILLA DE VISSEN WANTS TO WORK TOGETHER?
OF COURSE! WHY NOT? WHO DO YOU TAKE ME FOR? THIS ISN'T A COMPETITION!
"FOR EACH THAT ARRIVES, THERE'S ANOTHER THAT STARTS. AT THE STRANGE INN WE EAT: THE VIEW SWAYS IN ALL PARTS. A DRAWER IN THE CORNER CAN CRADLE ALL CHARTS. FIRST START AT NORTHWEST, THEN TO EAST GO APART, GO NORTHEAST, THEN NORTHWEST AND THEN FOLLOW YOUR HEART." WHAT COULD THAT MEAN?
IT'S DEFINITELY TALKING ABOUT AN INN, BUT AS FOR THE REST...IT ALMOST SEEMS LIKE IT'S TALKING ABOUT THE SEA...
OF COURSE! THE SWAYING OF THE SHIPS THROUGH THE WINDOW..."AT THE STRANGE INN WE EAT!" IT'S TALKING ABOUT THE TAVERN ACROSS FROM THE PORT!
I WAS SURE YOU'D DO THE WORK FOR ME! CONNIE, ZOE, ALICIA, WITH ME! AND YOU, TOO, VIC!
HEY, I DON'T WANT TO GO WITH YOU!
"WHO DO YOU TAKE ME FOR," EH? I SHOULD HAVE EXPECTED THIS!
YEAH...EVERYTHING'S A COMPETITION FOR ME, SWEETIE! A COMPETITION I'LL WIN!
OH, YOU'RE SUCH A DRAG, LITTLE SISTER!

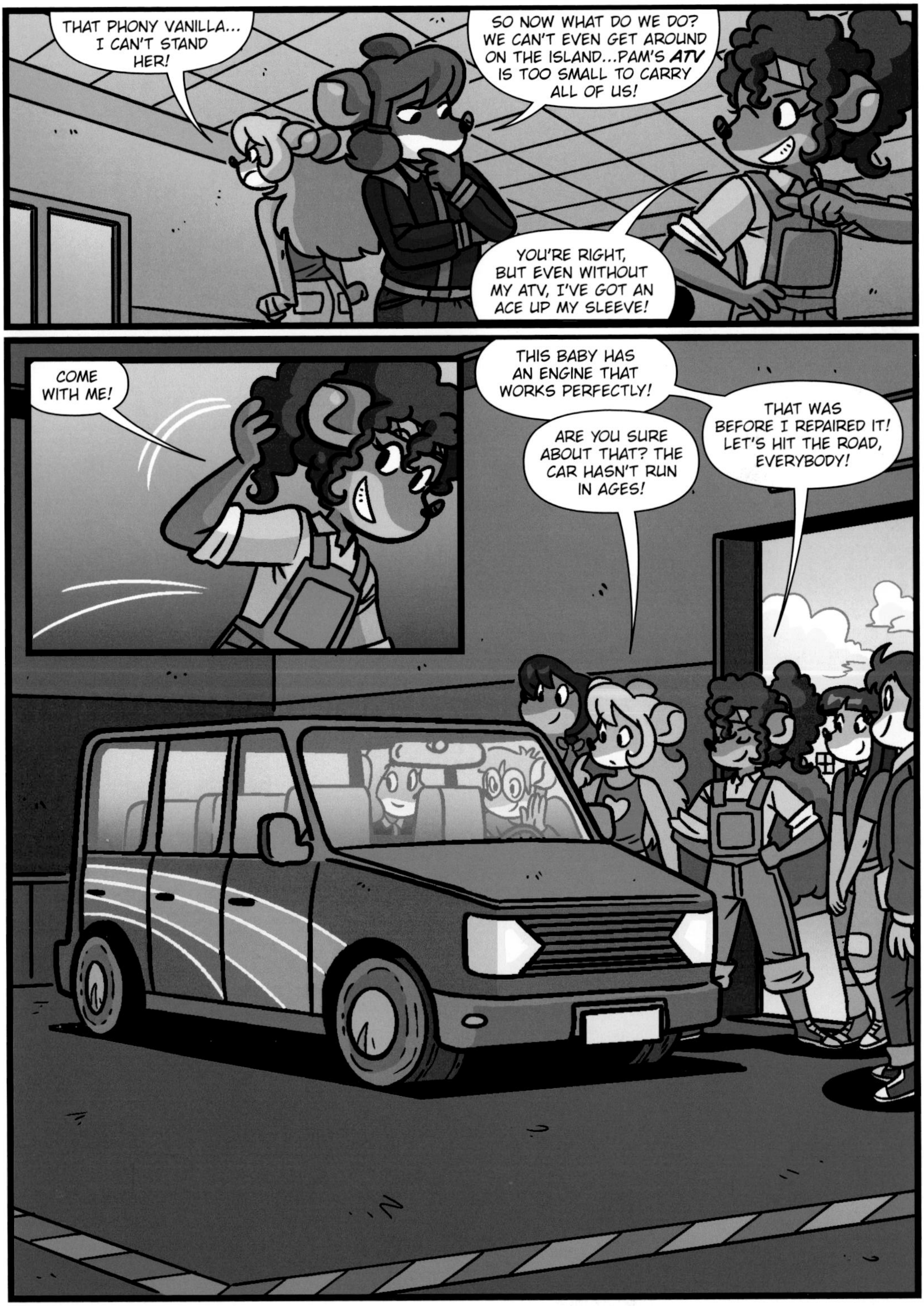
THAT PHONY VANILLA... I CAN'T STAND HER!
SO NOW WHAT DO WE DO? WE CAN'T EVEN GET AROUND ON THE ISLAND...PAM'S ATV IS TOO SMALL TO CARRY ALL OF US!
YOU'RE RIGHT, BUT EVEN WITHOUT MY ATV, I'VE GOT AN ACE UP MY SLEEVE!
COME WITH ME!
THIS BABY HAS AN ENGINE THAT WORKS PERFECTLY!
ARE YOU SURE ABOUT THAT? THE CAR HASN'T RUN IN AGES!
THAT WAS BEFORE I REPAIRED IT! LET'S HIT THE ROAD, EVERYBODY!

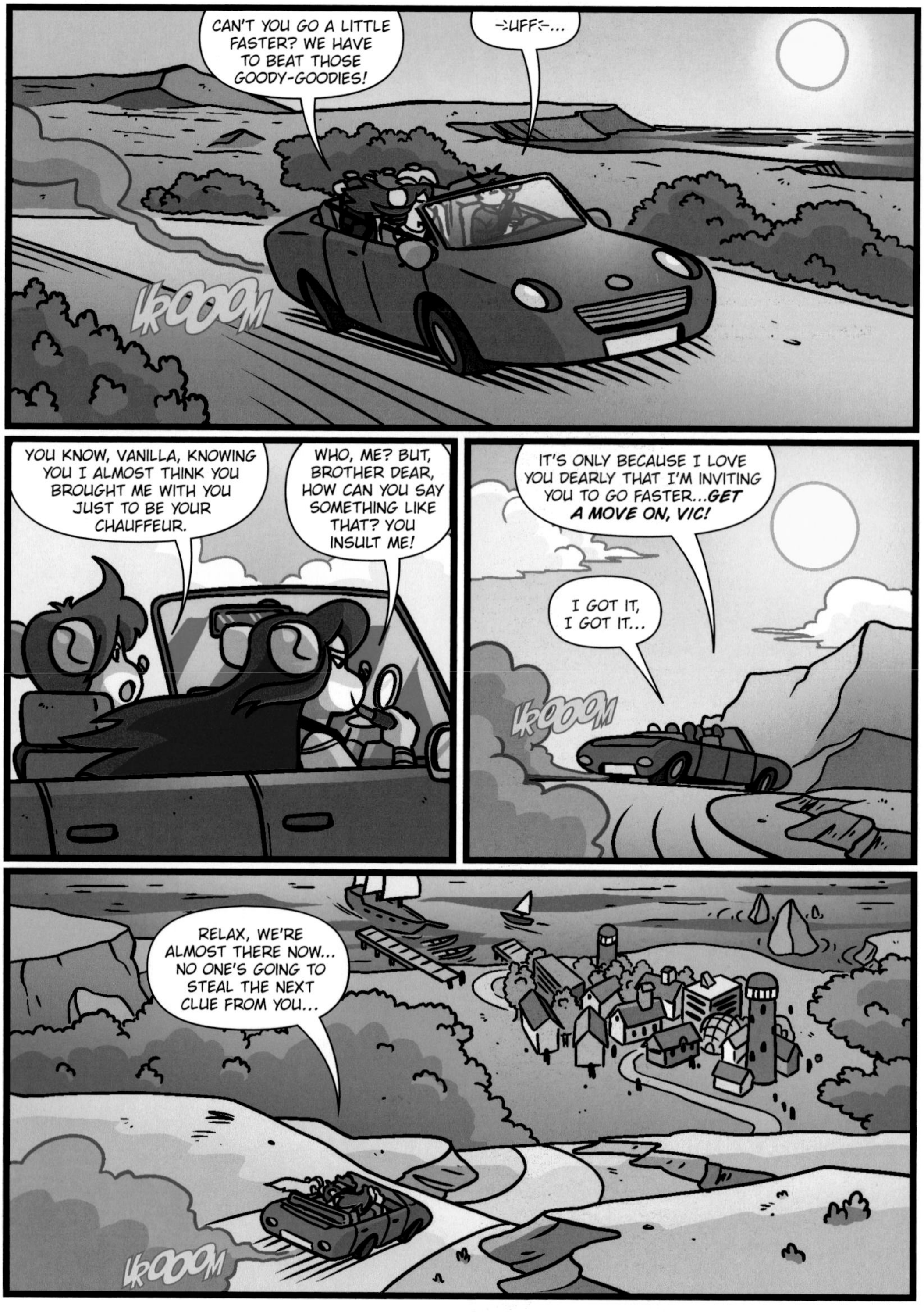
CAN'T YOU GO A LITTLE FASTER? WE HAVE TO BEAT THOSE GOODY-GOODIES!
-UFF-...
VROOOM
YOU KNOW, VANILLA, KNOWING YOU I ALMOST THINK YOU BROUGHT ME WITH YOU JUST TO BE YOUR CHAUFFEUR.
WHO, ME? BUT, BROTHER DEAR, HOW CAN YOU SAY SOMETHING LIKE THAT? YOU INSULT ME!
IT'S ONLY BECAUSE I LOVE YOU DEARLY THAT I'M INVITING YOU TO GO FASTER...GET A MOVE ON, VIC!
I GOT IT, I GOT IT...
VROOOM
RELAX, WE'RE ALMOST THERE NOW... NO ONE'S GOING TO STEAL THE NEXT CLUE FROM YOU...
VROOOM

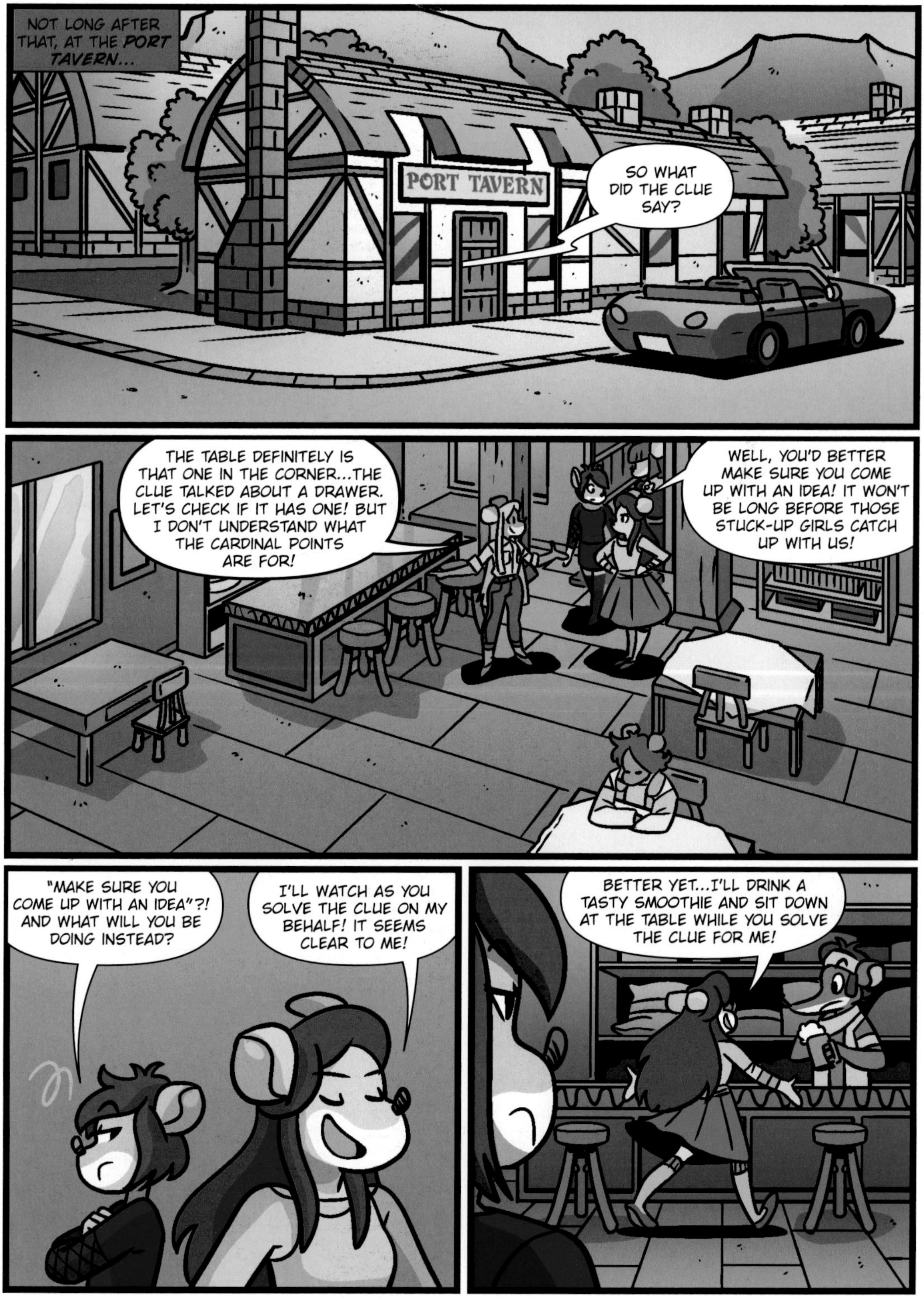
NOT LONG AFTER THAT, AT THE PORT TAVERN...
PORT TAVERN
SO WHAT DID THE CLUE SAY?
THE TABLE DEFINITELY IS THAT ONE IN THE CORNER...THE CLUE TALKED ABOUT A DRAWER. LET'S CHECK IF IT HAS ONE! BUT I DON'T UNDERSTAND WHAT THE CARDINAL POINTS ARE FOR!
WELL, YOU'D BETTER MAKE SURE YOU COME UP WITH AN IDEA! IT WON'T BE LONG BEFORE THOSE STUCK-UP GIRLS CATCH UP WITH US!
"MAKE SURE YOU COME UP WITH AN IDEA"?! AND WHAT WILL YOU BE DOING INSTEAD?
I'LL WATCH AS YOU SOLVE THE CLUE ON MY BEHALF! IT SEEMS CLEAR TO ME!
BETTER YET...I'LL DRINK A TASTY SMOOTHIE AND SIT DOWN AT THE TABLE WHILE YOU SOLVE THE CLUE FOR ME!

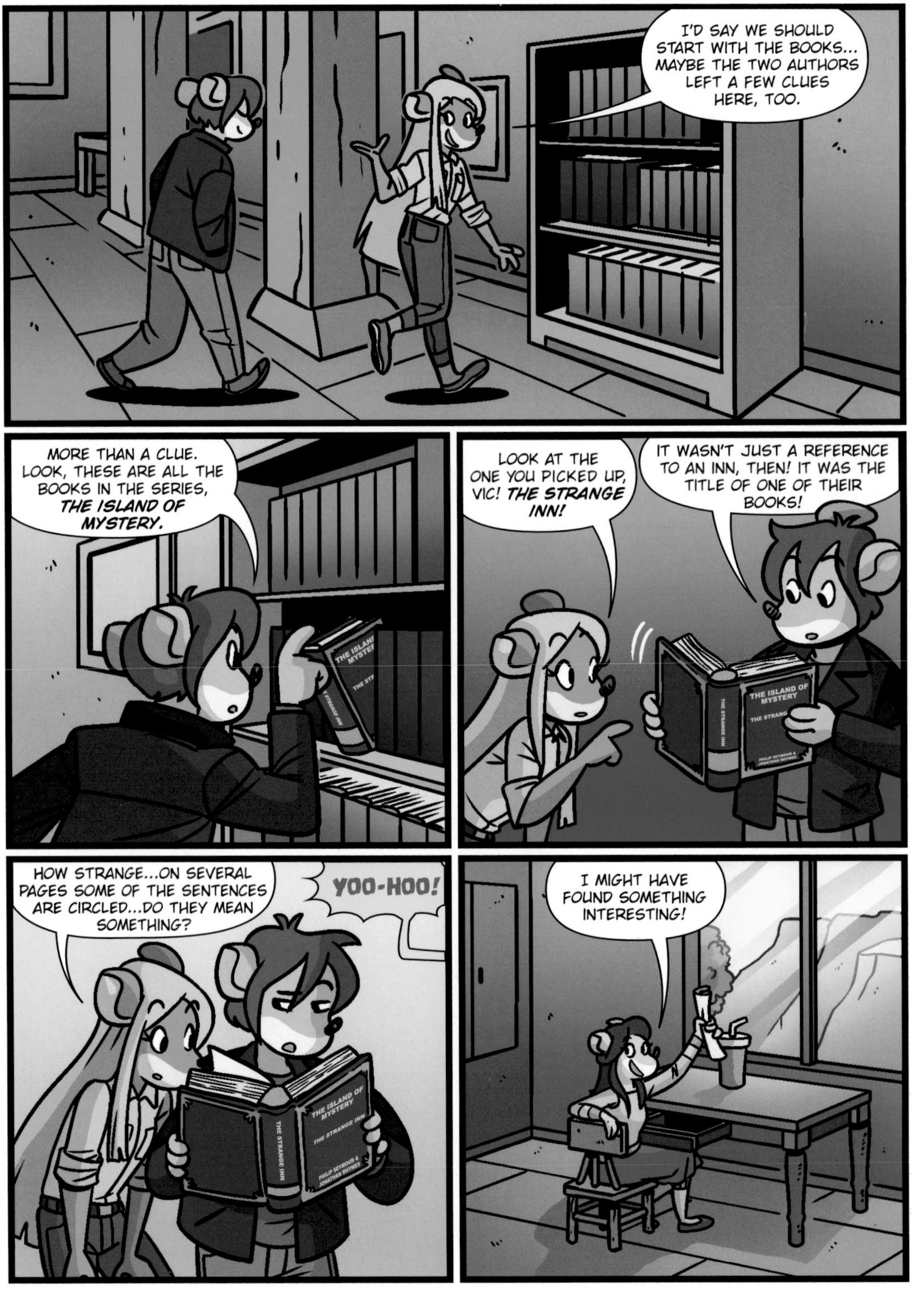
I'D SAY WE SHOULD START WITH THE BOOKS... MAYBE THE TWO AUTHORS LEFT A FEW CLUES HERE, TOO.
MORE THAN A CLUE. LOOK, THESE ARE ALL THE BOOKS IN THE SERIES, *THE ISLAND OF MYSTERY.*
THE ISLAND OF MYSTERY
THE STRANGE INN
LOOK AT THE ONE YOU PICKED UP, VIC! *THE STRANGE INN!*
IT WASN'T JUST A REFERENCE TO AN INN, THEN! IT WAS THE TITLE OF ONE OF THEIR BOOKS!
HOW STRANGE...ON SEVERAL PAGES SOME OF THE SENTENCES ARE CIRCLED...DO THEY MEAN SOMETHING?
YOO-HOO!
THE ISLAND OF MYSTERY
THE STRANGE INN
PHILIP SEYMOUR & JONATHAN RHYMES
I MIGHT HAVE FOUND SOMETHING INTERESTING!

THEY'RE NUMBERS! LAID OUT IN THE CARDINAL POINTS, LIKE ON A COMPASS.

ZOE, YOU'RE A GENIUS!

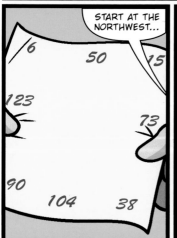

START AT THE NORTHWEST...

VIC, GO TO PAGE 6!

PAGE 6...

THERE'S SOME TEXT CIRCLED. IT SAYS, "YOU NEED THE COURAGE OF A LION."

was a beautifu
sorcerous, a closet, an
a beast with a mane. O
was it a man made of r
and one with hay for br
Nevertheless, the young
child protagonist said,
"You need the courage
of a lion!"

6

I FEEL LIKE WE'RE ON THE RIGHT PATH! THE NEXT COORDINATE... "TO EAST GO APART"... PAGE 73!

ANOTHER LINE IS CIRCLED..."TO WATCH A STAR..."

THE ISLAND MYSTERY
THE STRANG

THE STRANG

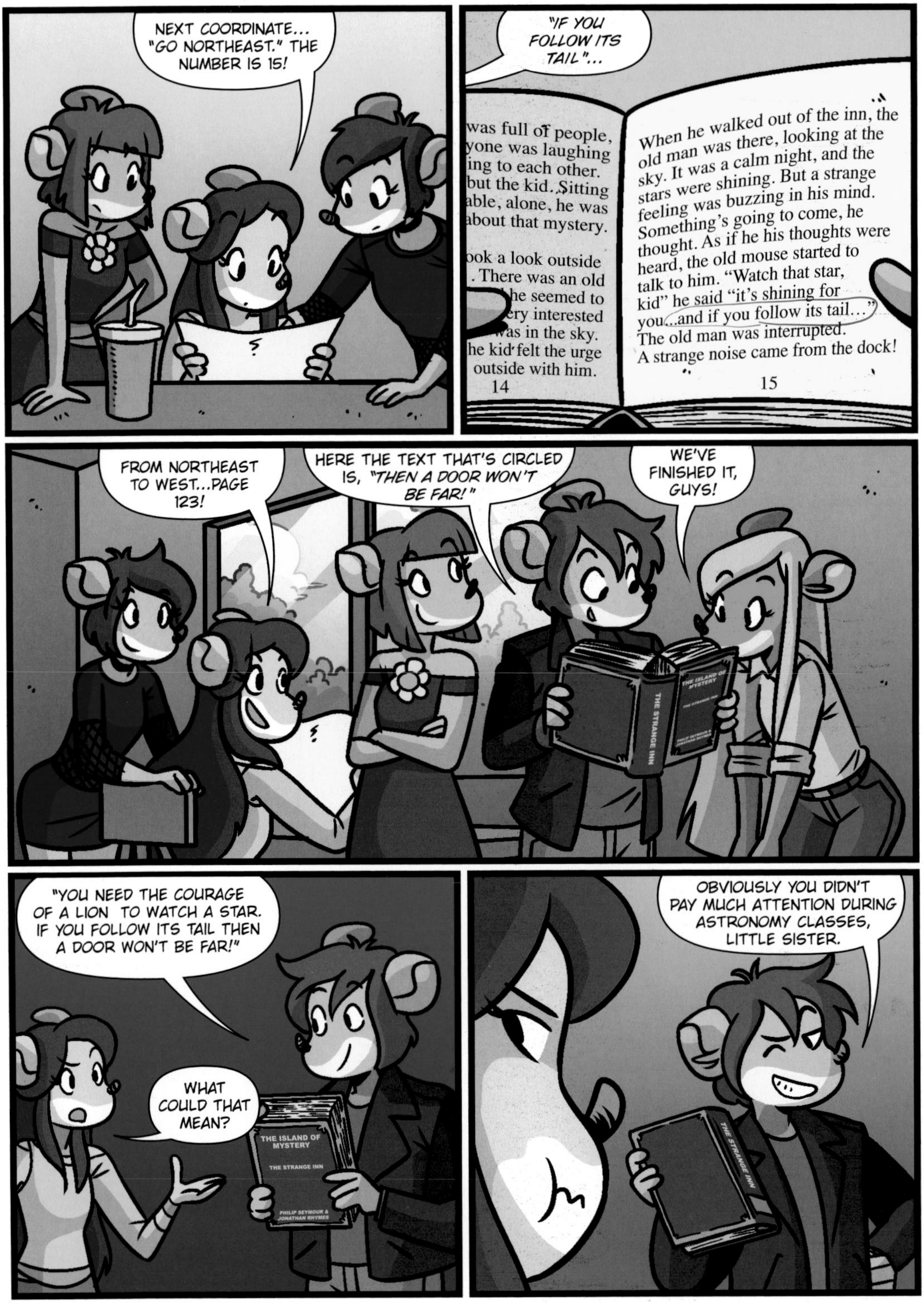
NEXT COORDINATE... "GO NORTHEAST." THE NUMBER IS 15!
"IF YOU FOLLOW ITS TAIL"...
was full of people,
yone was laughing
ing to each other.
but the kid. Sitting
able, alone, he was
about that mystery.
ook a look outside
. There was an old
he seemed to
ery interested
was in the sky.
he kid felt the urge
outside with him.
14
When he walked out of the inn, the old man was there, looking at the sky. It was a calm night, and the stars were shining. But a strange feeling was buzzing in his mind. Something's going to come, he thought. As if he his thoughts were heard, the old mouse started to talk to him. "Watch that star, kid" he said "it's shining for you...and if you follow its tail..." The old man was interrupted. A strange noise came from the dock!
15
FROM NORTHEAST TO WEST...PAGE 123!
HERE THE TEXT THAT'S CIRCLED IS, "THEN A DOOR WON'T BE FAR!"
WE'VE FINISHED IT, GUYS!
THE ISLAND OF MYSTERY
THE STRANGE INN
"YOU NEED THE COURAGE OF A LION TO WATCH A STAR. IF YOU FOLLOW ITS TAIL THEN A DOOR WON'T BE FAR!"
WHAT COULD THAT MEAN?
THE ISLAND OF MYSTERY
THE STRANGE INN
PHILIP SEYMOUR & JONATHAN RHYMES
OBVIOUSLY YOU DIDN'T PAY MUCH ATTENTION DURING ASTRONOMY CLASSES, LITTLE SISTER.
THE STRANGE INN

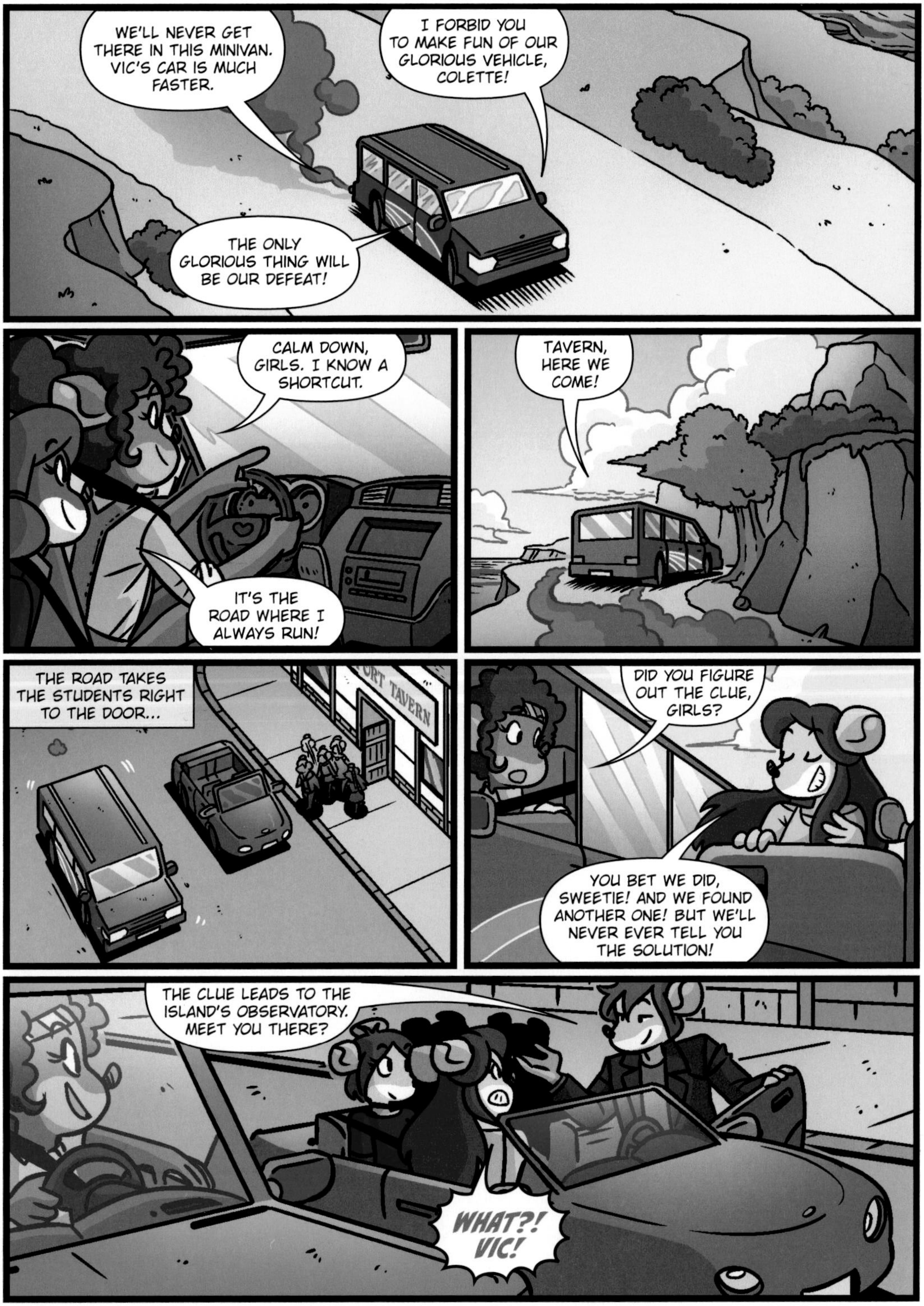

WE'LL NEVER GET THERE IN THIS MINIVAN. VIC'S CAR IS MUCH FASTER.
I FORBID YOU TO MAKE FUN OF OUR GLORIOUS VEHICLE, COLETTE!
THE ONLY GLORIOUS THING WILL BE OUR DEFEAT!
CALM DOWN, GIRLS. I KNOW A SHORTCUT.
IT'S THE ROAD WHERE I ALWAYS RUN!
TAVERN, HERE WE COME!
THE ROAD TAKES THE STUDENTS RIGHT TO THE DOOR...
DID YOU FIGURE OUT THE CLUE, GIRLS?
YOU BET WE DID, SWEETIE! AND WE FOUND ANOTHER ONE! BUT WE'LL NEVER EVER TELL YOU THE SOLUTION!
THE CLUE LEADS TO THE ISLAND'S OBSERVATORY. MEET YOU THERE?
WHAT?! VIC!

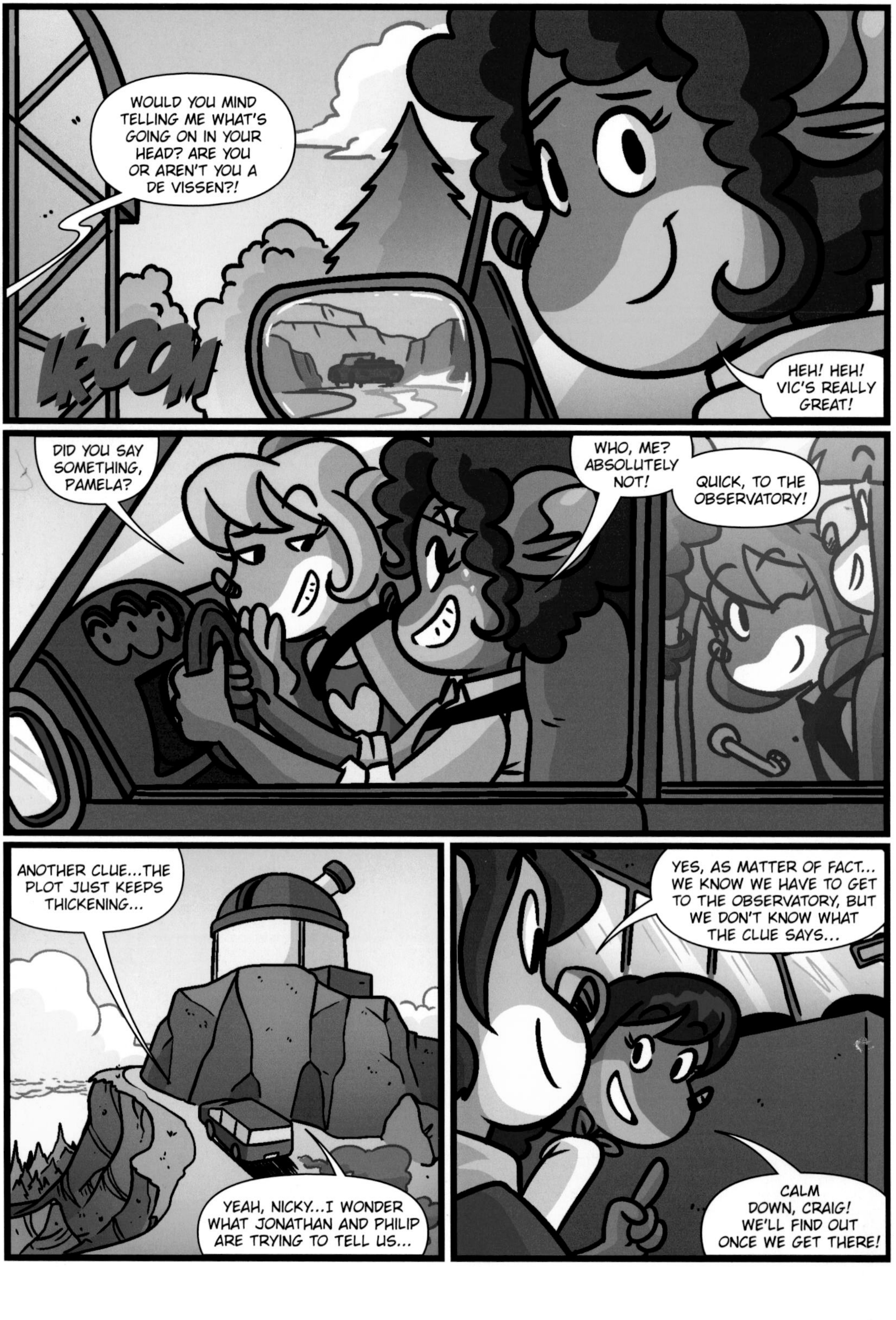
WOULD YOU MIND TELLING ME WHAT'S GOING ON IN YOUR HEAD? ARE YOU OR AREN'T YOU A DE VISSEN?!
VROOM
HEH! HEH! VIC'S REALLY GREAT!
DID YOU SAY SOMETHING, PAMELA?
WHO, ME? ABSOLUTELY NOT!
QUICK, TO THE OBSERVATORY!
ANOTHER CLUE...THE PLOT JUST KEEPS THICKENING...
YEAH, NICKY...I WONDER WHAT JONATHAN AND PHILIP ARE TRYING TO TELL US...
YES, AS MATTER OF FACT... WE KNOW WE HAVE TO GET TO THE OBSERVATORY, BUT WE DON'T KNOW WHAT THE CLUE SAYS...
CALM DOWN, CRAIG! WE'LL FIND OUT ONCE WE GET THERE!

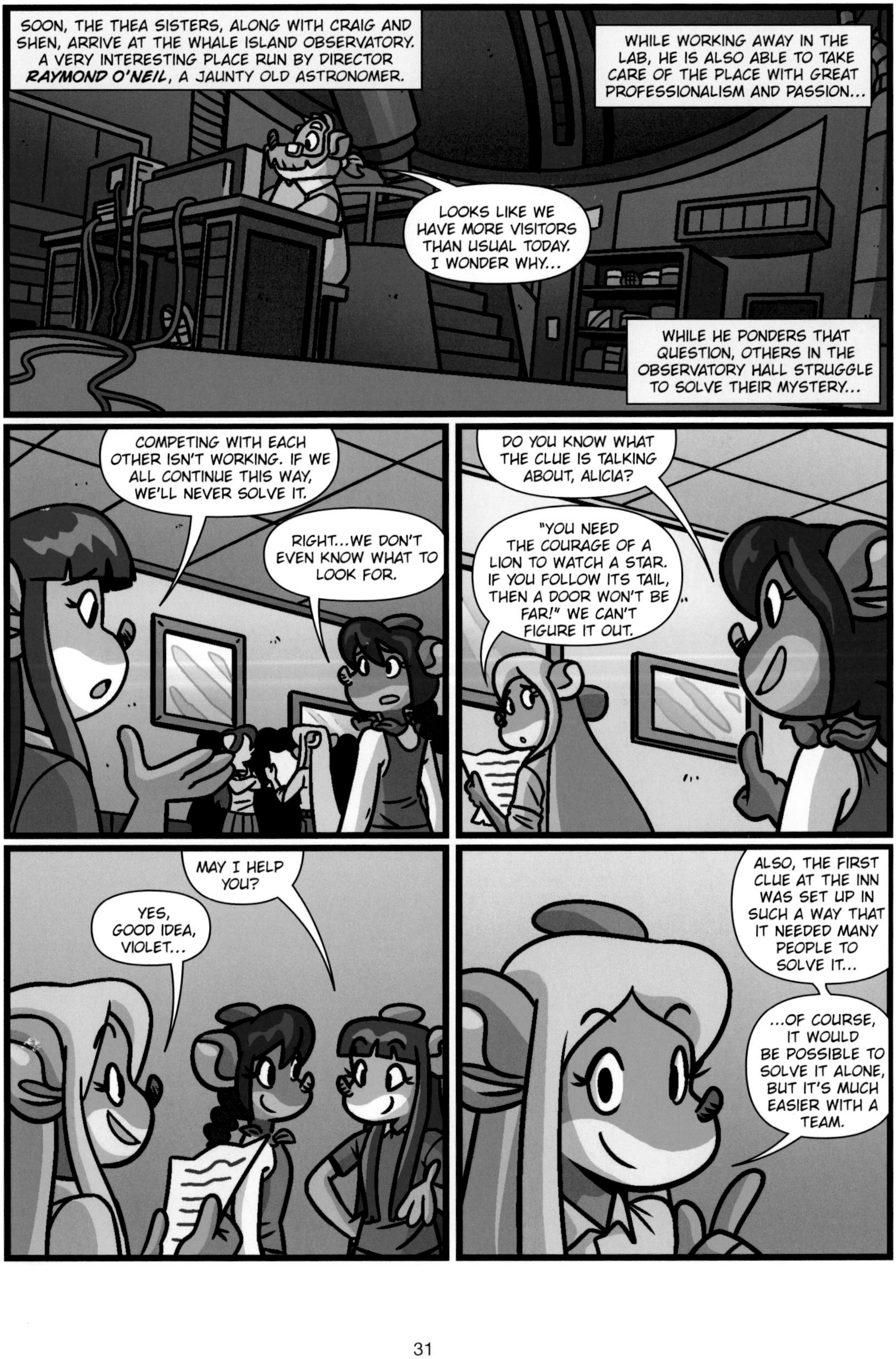
SOON, THE THEA SISTERS, ALONG WITH CRAIG AND SHEN, ARRIVE AT THE WHALE ISLAND OBSERVATORY. A VERY INTERESTING PLACE RUN BY DIRECTOR RAYMOND O'NEIL, A JAUNTY OLD ASTRONOMER.
WHILE WORKING AWAY IN THE LAB, HE IS ALSO ABLE TO TAKE CARE OF THE PLACE WITH GREAT PROFESSIONALISM AND PASSION...
LOOKS LIKE WE HAVE MORE VISITORS THAN USUAL TODAY. I WONDER WHY...
WHILE HE PONDERS THAT QUESTION, OTHERS IN THE OBSERVATORY HALL STRUGGLE TO SOLVE THEIR MYSTERY...
COMPETING WITH EACH OTHER ISN'T WORKING. IF WE ALL CONTINUE THIS WAY, WE'LL NEVER SOLVE IT.
RIGHT...WE DON'T EVEN KNOW WHAT TO LOOK FOR.
DO YOU KNOW WHAT THE CLUE IS TALKING ABOUT, ALICIA?
"YOU NEED THE COURAGE OF A LION TO WATCH A STAR. IF YOU FOLLOW ITS TAIL, THEN A DOOR WON'T BE FAR!" WE CAN'T FIGURE IT OUT.
MAY I HELP YOU?
YES, GOOD IDEA, VIOLET...
ALSO, THE FIRST CLUE AT THE INN WAS SET UP IN SUCH A WAY THAT IT NEEDED MANY PEOPLE TO SOLVE IT...
...OF COURSE, IT WOULD BE POSSIBLE TO SOLVE IT ALONE, BUT IT'S MUCH EASIER WITH A TEAM.

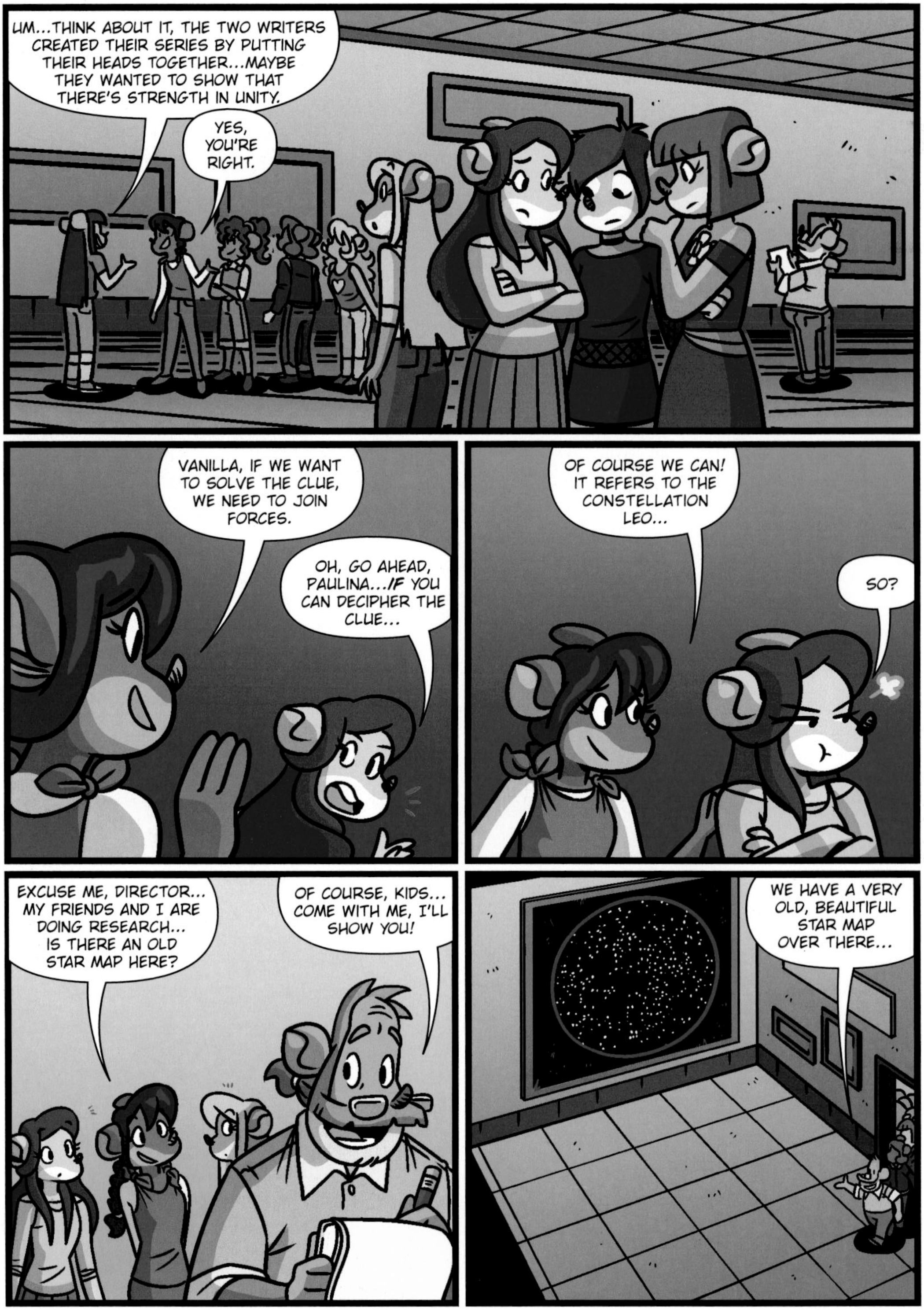
UM...THINK ABOUT IT, THE TWO WRITERS CREATED THEIR SERIES BY PUTTING THEIR HEADS TOGETHER...MAYBE THEY WANTED TO SHOW THAT THERE'S STRENGTH IN UNITY.
YES, YOU'RE RIGHT.
VANILLA, IF WE WANT TO SOLVE THE CLUE, WE NEED TO JOIN FORCES.
OH, GO AHEAD, PAULINA...*IF* YOU CAN DECIPHER THE CLUE...
OF COURSE WE CAN! IT REFERS TO THE CONSTELLATION LEO...
SO?
EXCUSE ME, DIRECTOR... MY FRIENDS AND I ARE DOING RESEARCH... IS THERE AN OLD STAR MAP HERE?
OF COURSE, KIDS... COME WITH ME, I'LL SHOW YOU!
WE HAVE A VERY OLD, BEAUTIFUL STAR MAP OVER THERE...

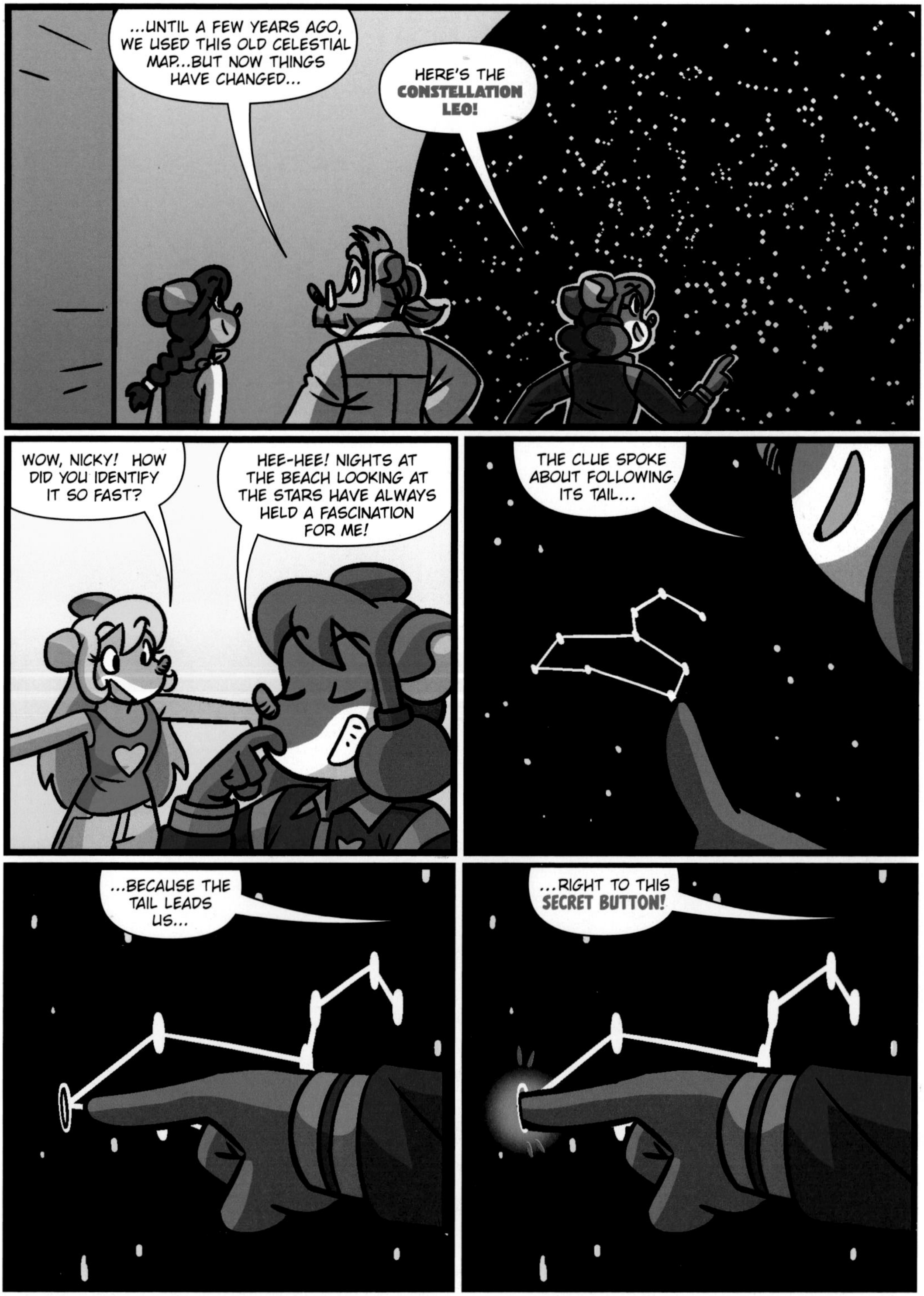
...UNTIL A FEW YEARS AGO, WE USED THIS OLD CELESTIAL MAP...BUT NOW THINGS HAVE CHANGED...
HERE'S THE **CONSTELLATION LEO!**
WOW, NICKY! HOW DID YOU IDENTIFY IT SO FAST?
HEE-HEE! NIGHTS AT THE BEACH LOOKING AT THE STARS HAVE ALWAYS HELD A FASCINATION FOR ME!
THE CLUE SPOKE ABOUT FOLLOWING ITS TAIL...
...BECAUSE THE TAIL LEADS US...
...RIGHT TO THIS **SECRET BUTTON!**

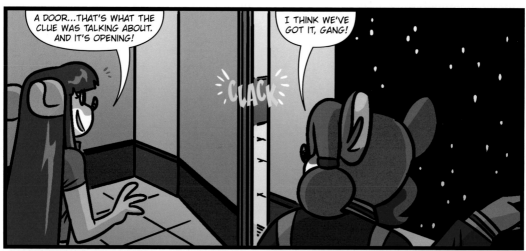

A DOOR...THAT'S WHAT THE CLUE WAS TALKING ABOUT. AND IT'S OPENING!

CLACK

I THINK WE'VE GOT IT, GANG!

HERE IT IS! I DON'T CARE ABOUT ALL THIS DUST, AS LONG AS IT LEADS ME--I, MEAN US--

--TO THE **TREASURE!**

LOOK! I GOT IT OPEN!

AND YOU DID IT ALL BY YOURSELF, TOO!

IT'S JUST ANOTHER DUMB CLUE...

"IT TAKES THE RIGHT LIGHT TO SHOW THE DEEP BLUE, BUT TO MOVE THE LEFT WING TAKES A ROCK, IT'S TRUE!"

THE RIGHT LIGHT CAN SHOW THE DEEP BLUE... THE ISLAND LIGHTHOUSE!

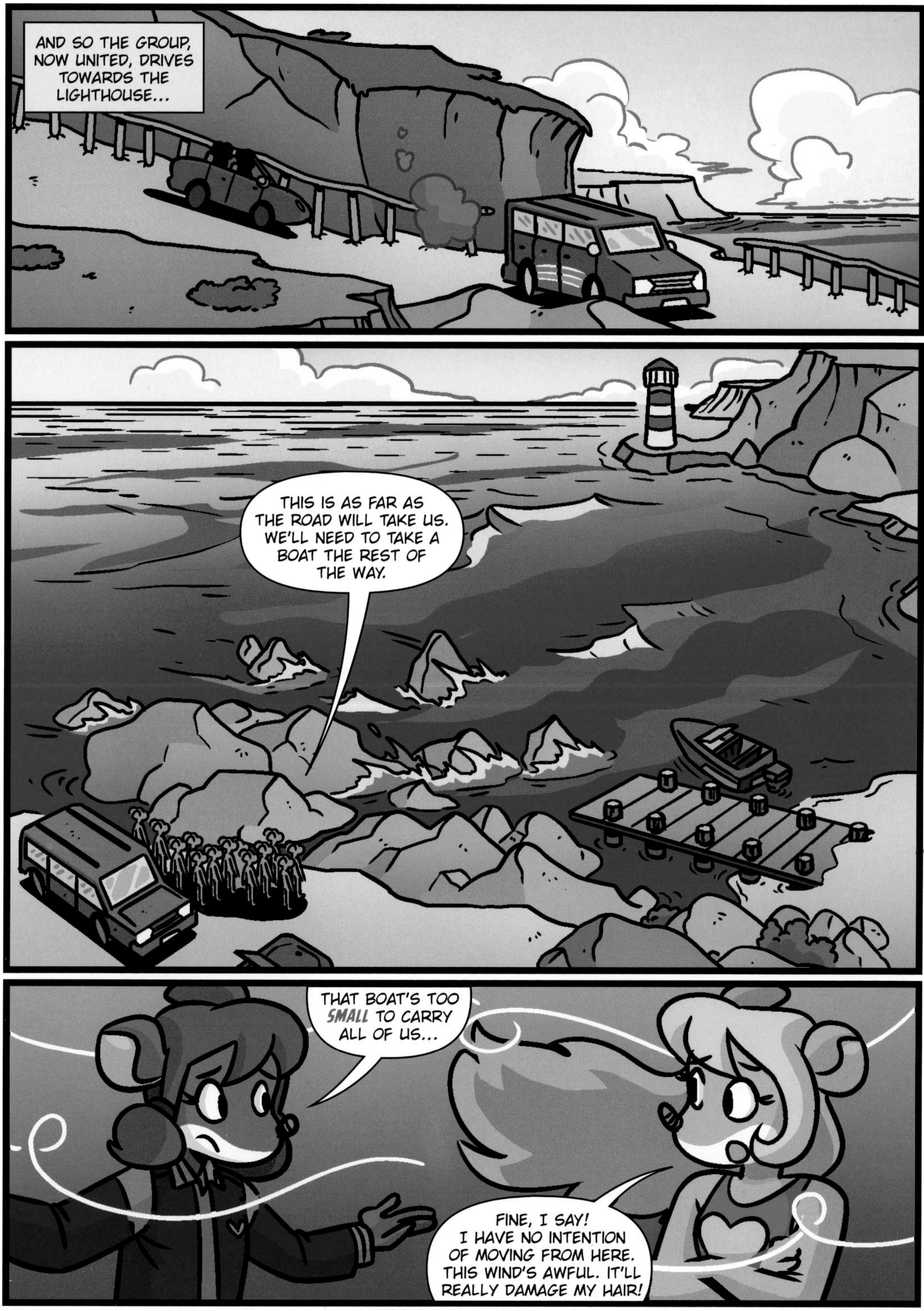
AND SO THE GROUP, NOW UNITED, DRIVES TOWARDS THE LIGHTHOUSE...
THIS IS AS FAR AS THE ROAD WILL TAKE US. WE'LL NEED TO TAKE A BOAT THE REST OF THE WAY.
THAT BOAT'S TOO SMALL TO CARRY ALL OF US...
FINE, I SAY! I HAVE NO INTENTION OF MOVING FROM HERE. THIS WIND'S AWFUL. IT'LL REALLY DAMAGE MY HAIR!

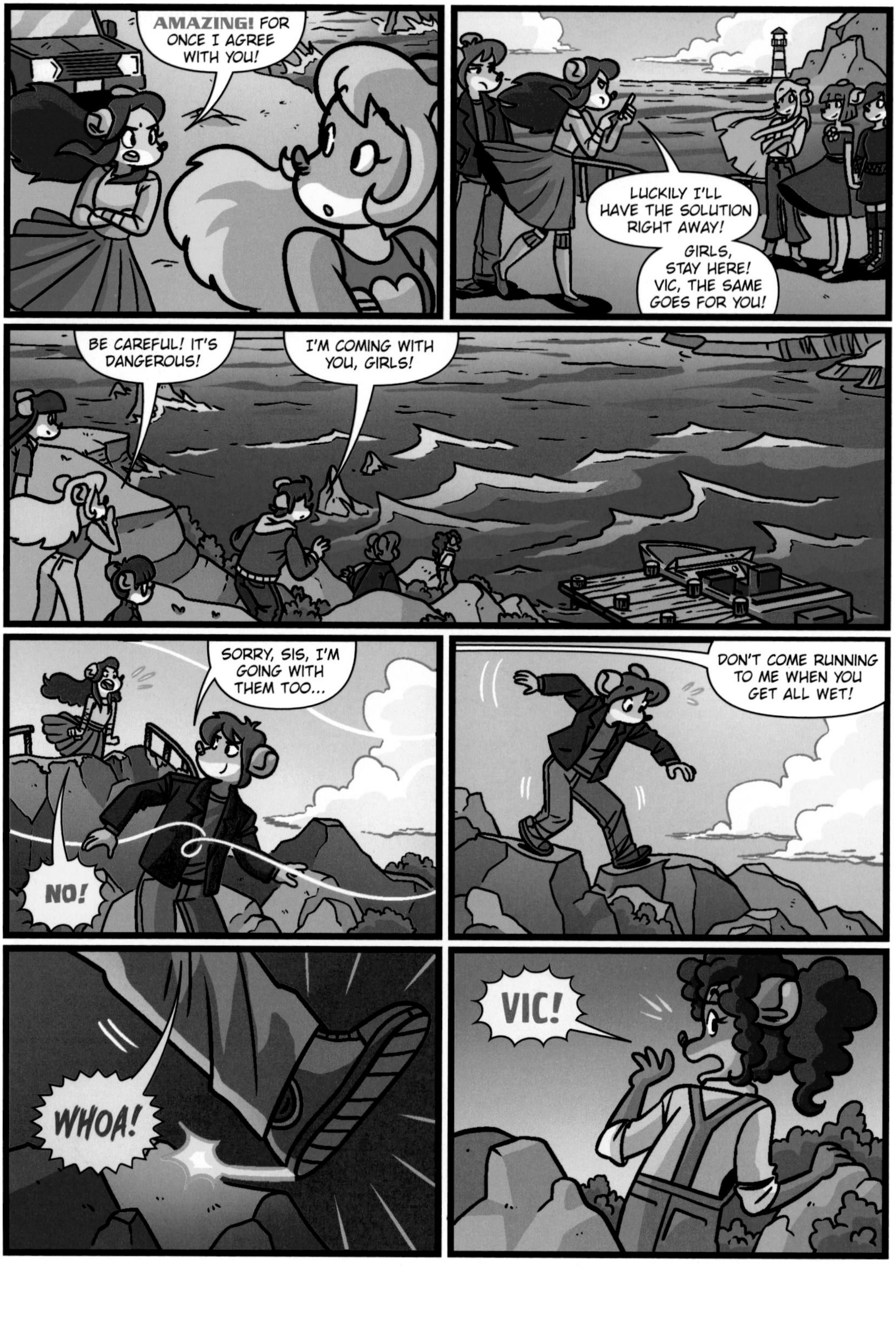
AMAZING! FOR ONCE I AGREE WITH YOU!
LUCKILY I'LL HAVE THE SOLUTION RIGHT AWAY!
GIRLS, STAY HERE! VIC, THE SAME GOES FOR YOU!
BE CAREFUL! IT'S DANGEROUS!
I'M COMING WITH YOU, GIRLS!
SORRY, SIS, I'M GOING WITH THEM TOO...
NO!
DON'T COME RUNNING TO ME WHEN YOU GET ALL WET!
WHOA!
VIC!

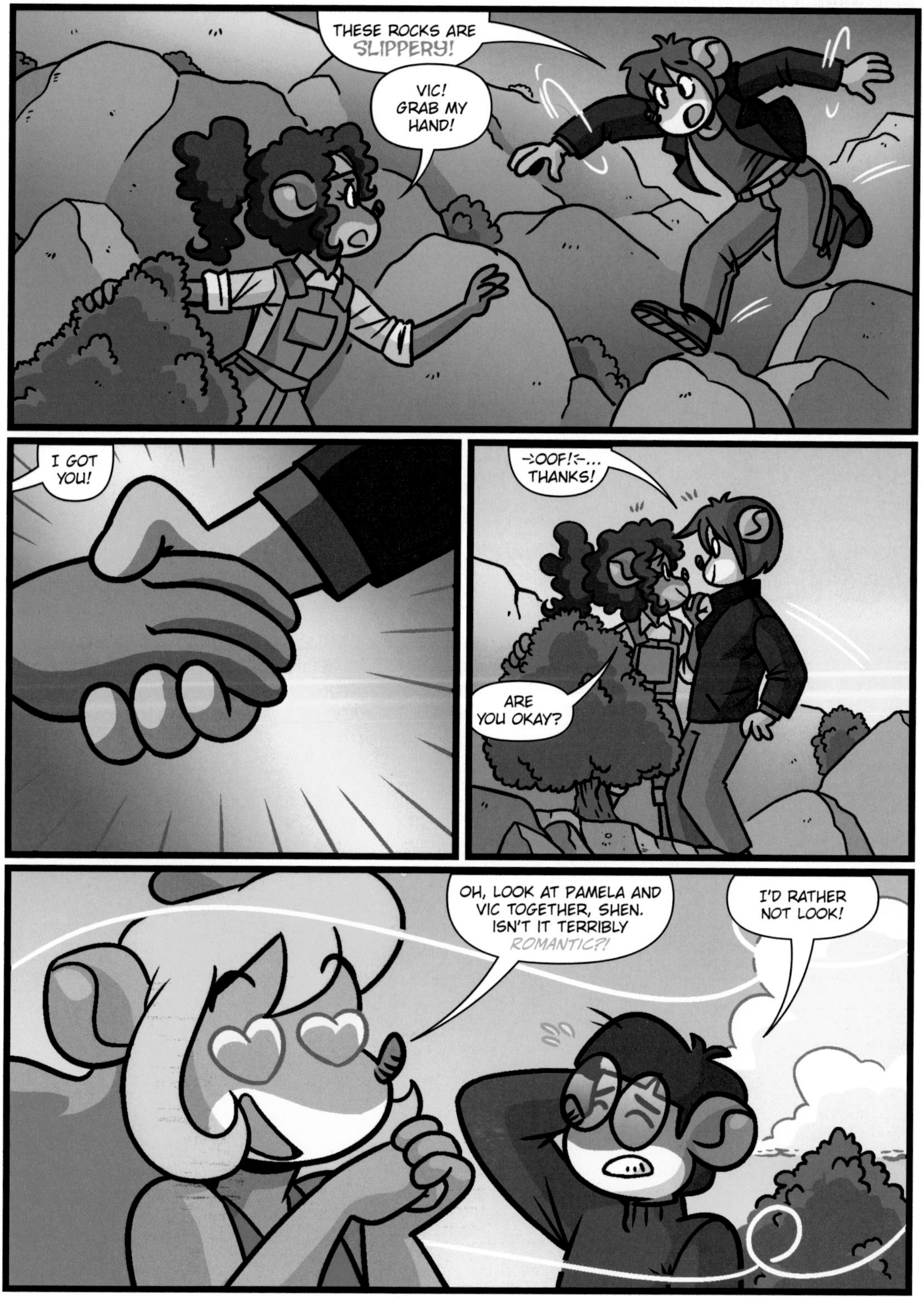
THESE ROCKS ARE SLIPPERY!
VIC! GRAB MY HAND!
I GOT YOU!
-OOF!-... THANKS!
ARE YOU OKAY?
OH, LOOK AT PAMELA AND VIC TOGETHER, SHEN. ISN'T IT TERRIBLY ROMANTIC?!
I'D RATHER NOT LOOK!

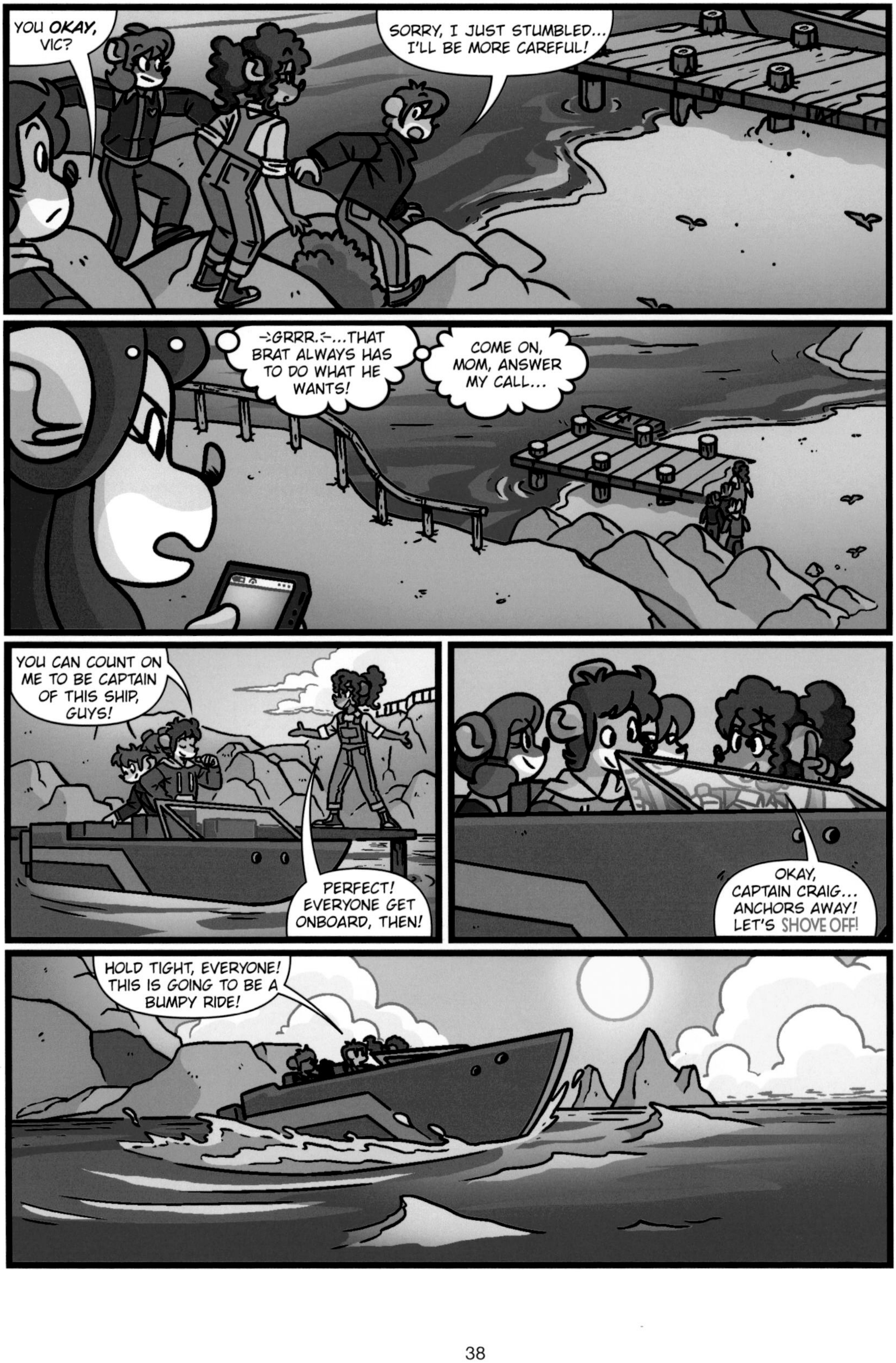

YOU OKAY, VIC?
SORRY, I JUST STUMBLED... I'LL BE MORE CAREFUL!
→GRRR.←...THAT BRAT ALWAYS HAS TO DO WHAT HE WANTS!
COME ON, MOM, ANSWER MY CALL...
YOU CAN COUNT ON ME TO BE CAPTAIN OF THIS SHIP, GUYS!
PERFECT! EVERYONE GET ONBOARD, THEN!
OKAY, CAPTAIN CRAIG... ANCHORS AWAY! LET'S SHOVE OFF!
HOLD TIGHT, EVERYONE! THIS IS GOING TO BE A BUMPY RIDE!

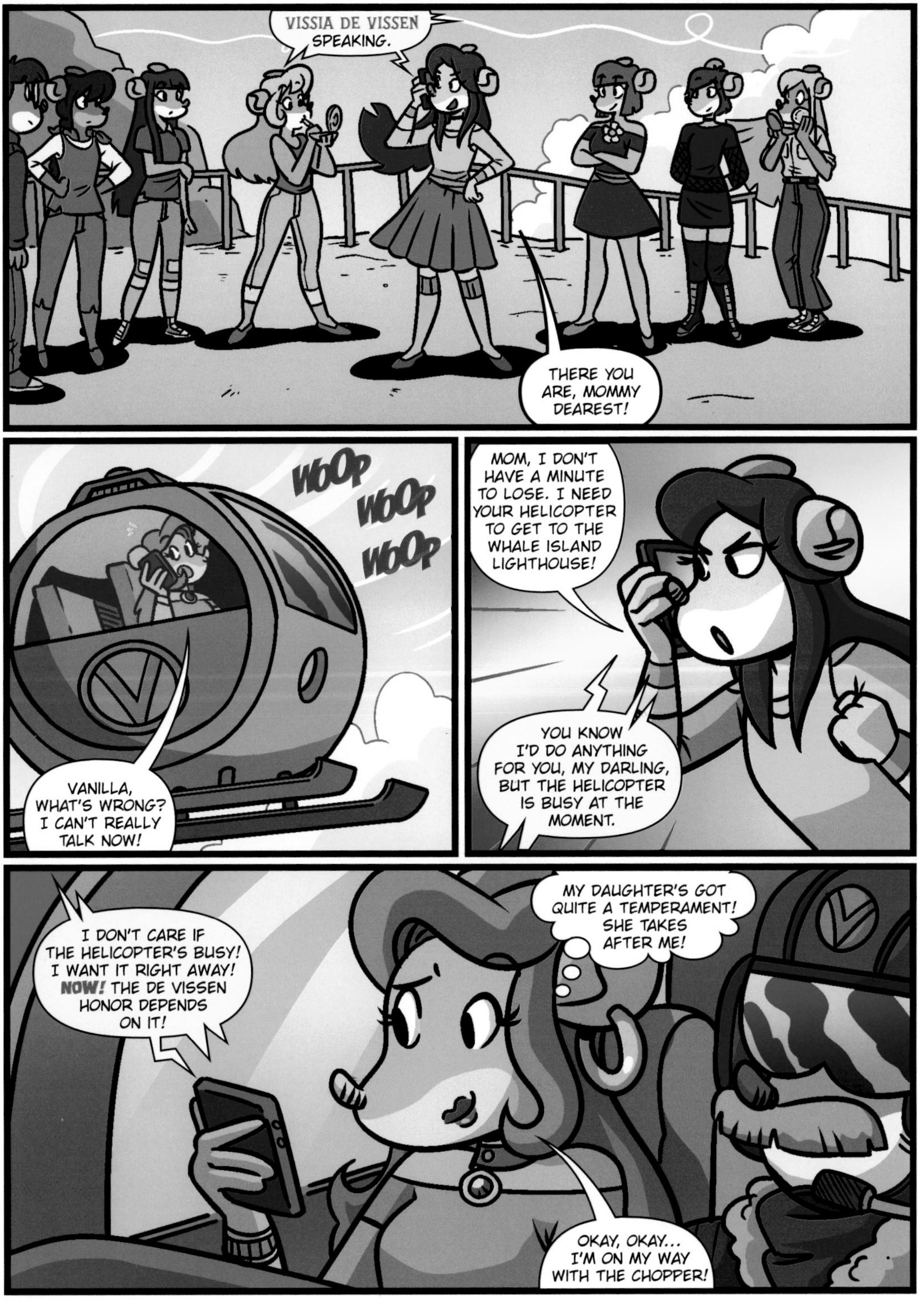
VISSIA DE VISSEN SPEAKING.
THERE YOU ARE, MOMMY DEAREST!
WOOP WOOP WOOP
VANILLA, WHAT'S WRONG? I CAN'T REALLY TALK NOW!
MOM, I DON'T HAVE A MINUTE TO LOSE. I NEED YOUR HELICOPTER TO GET TO THE WHALE ISLAND LIGHTHOUSE!
YOU KNOW I'D DO ANYTHING FOR YOU, MY DARLING, BUT THE HELICOPTER IS BUSY AT THE MOMENT.
I DON'T CARE IF THE HELICOPTER'S BUSY! I WANT IT RIGHT AWAY! NOW! THE DE VISSEN HONOR DEPENDS ON IT!
MY DAUGHTER'S GOT QUITE A TEMPERAMENT! SHE TAKES AFTER ME!
OKAY, OKAY... I'M ON MY WAY WITH THE CHOPPER!

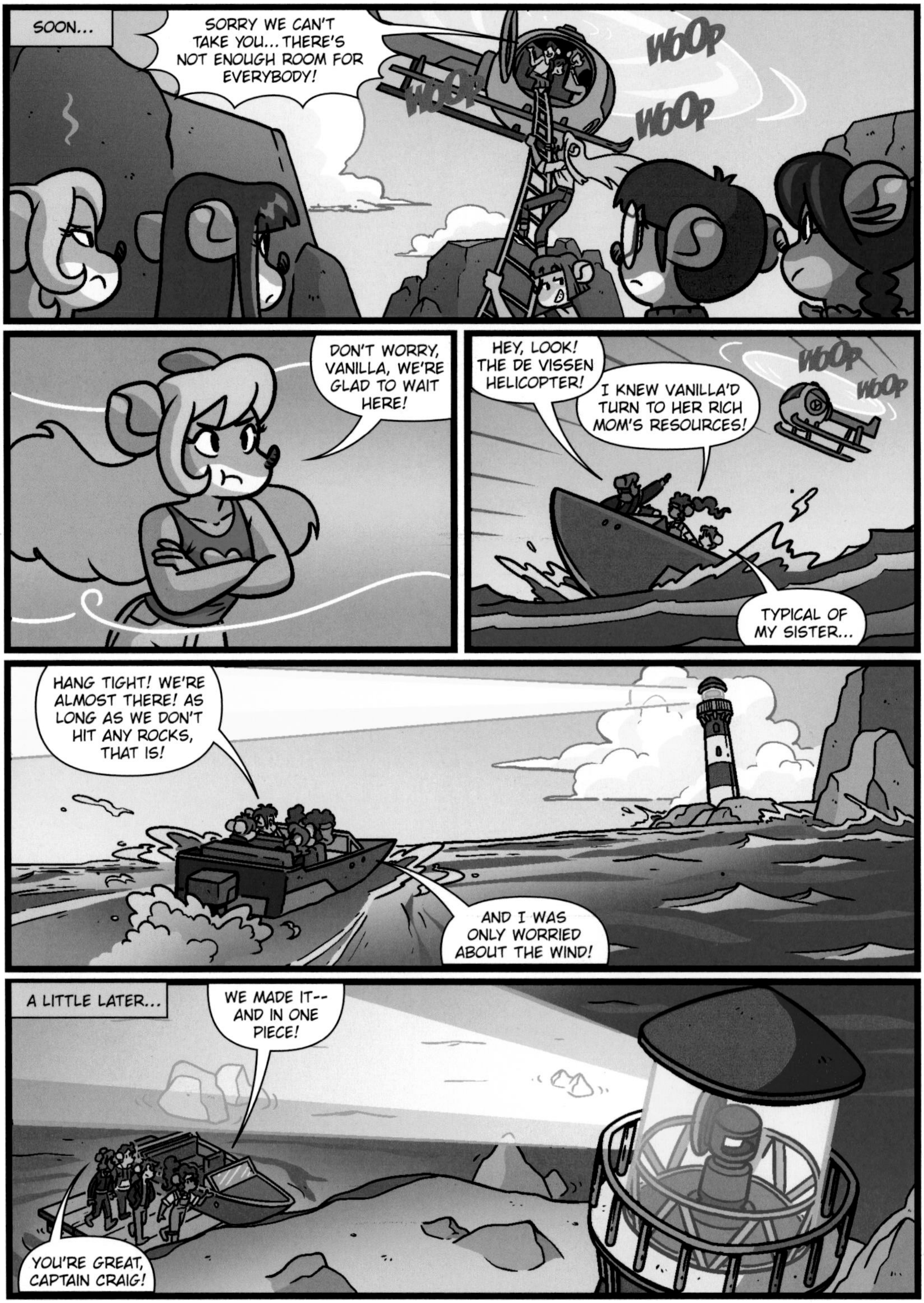
SOON...
SORRY WE CAN'T TAKE YOU... THERE'S NOT ENOUGH ROOM FOR EVERYBODY!
WOOP
WOOP
WOOP
DON'T WORRY, VANILLA, WE'RE GLAD TO WAIT HERE!
HEY, LOOK! THE DE VISSEN HELICOPTER!
I KNEW VANILLA'D TURN TO HER RICH MOM'S RESOURCES!
WOOP
WOOP
TYPICAL OF MY SISTER...
HANG TIGHT! WE'RE ALMOST THERE! AS LONG AS WE DON'T HIT ANY ROCKS, THAT IS!
AND I WAS ONLY WORRIED ABOUT THE WIND!
A LITTLE LATER...
WE MADE IT-- AND IN ONE PIECE!
YOU'RE GREAT, CAPTAIN CRAIG!

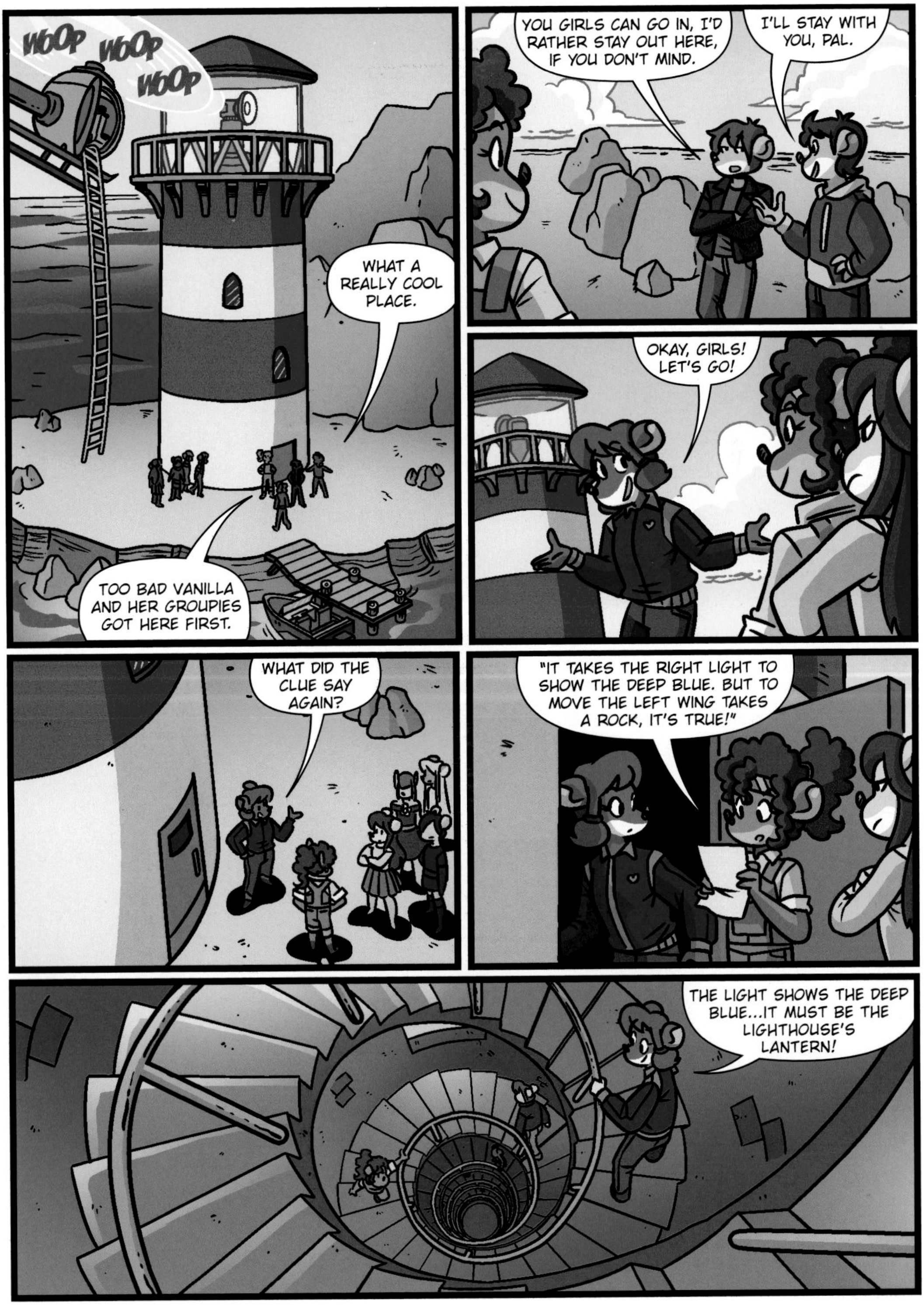
WOOP WOOP WOOP
WHAT A REALLY COOL PLACE.
TOO BAD VANILLA AND HER GROUPIES GOT HERE FIRST.
YOU GIRLS CAN GO IN, I'D RATHER STAY OUT HERE, IF YOU DON'T MIND.
I'LL STAY WITH YOU, PAL.
OKAY, GIRLS! LET'S GO!
WHAT DID THE CLUE SAY AGAIN?
"IT TAKES THE RIGHT LIGHT TO SHOW THE DEEP BLUE. BUT TO MOVE THE LEFT WING TAKES A ROCK, IT'S TRUE!"
THE LIGHT SHOWS THE DEEP BLUE...IT MUST BE THE LIGHTHOUSE'S LANTERN!

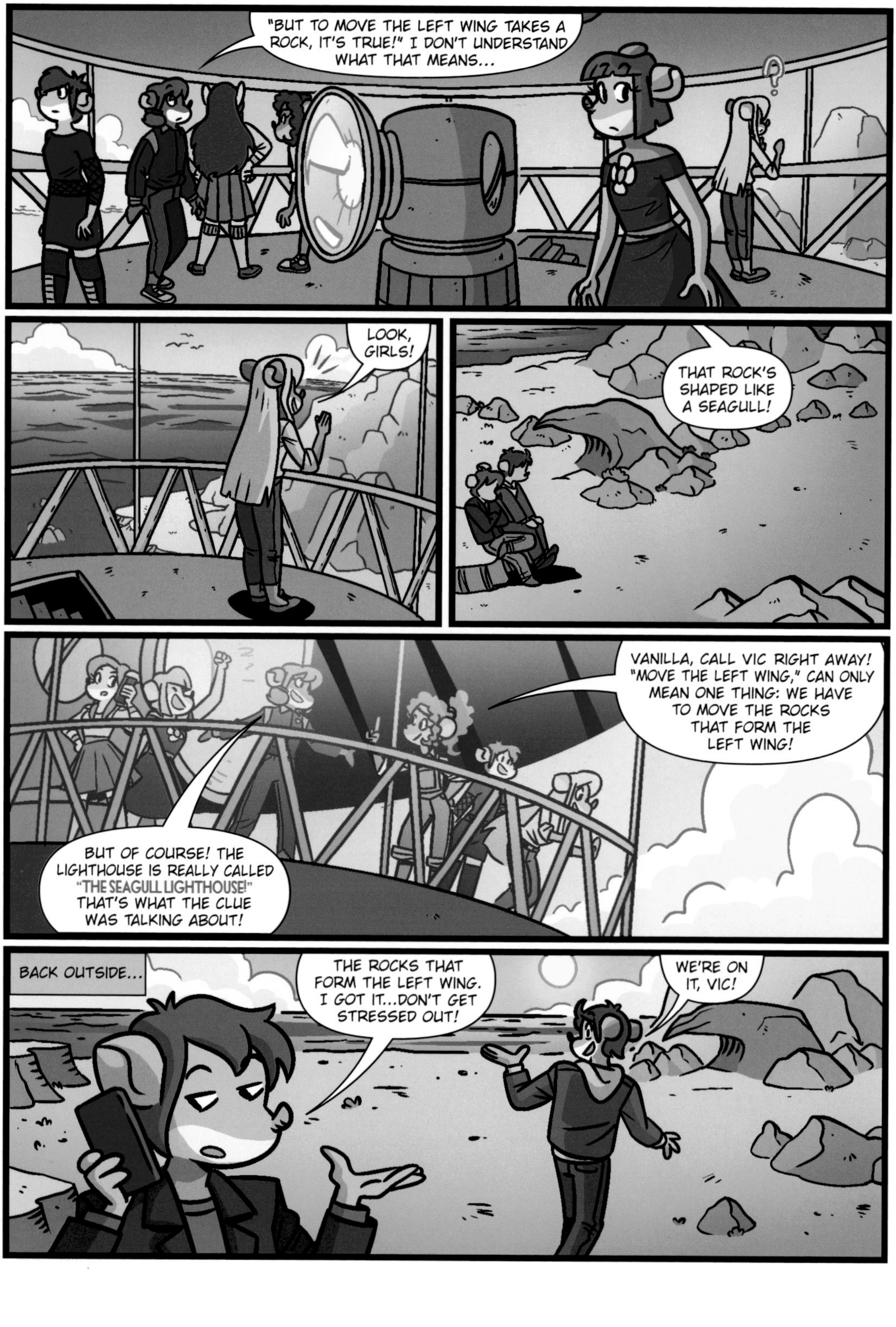
"BUT TO MOVE THE LEFT WING TAKES A ROCK, IT'S TRUE!" I DON'T UNDERSTAND WHAT THAT MEANS...
LOOK, GIRLS!
THAT ROCK'S SHAPED LIKE A SEAGULL!
VANILLA, CALL VIC RIGHT AWAY! "MOVE THE LEFT WING," CAN ONLY MEAN ONE THING: WE HAVE TO MOVE THE ROCKS THAT FORM THE LEFT WING!
BUT OF COURSE! THE LIGHTHOUSE IS REALLY CALLED "THE SEAGULL LIGHTHOUSE!" THAT'S WHAT THE CLUE WAS TALKING ABOUT!
BACK OUTSIDE...
THE ROCKS THAT FORM THE LEFT WING. I GOT IT...DON'T GET STRESSED OUT!
WE'RE ON IT, VIC!

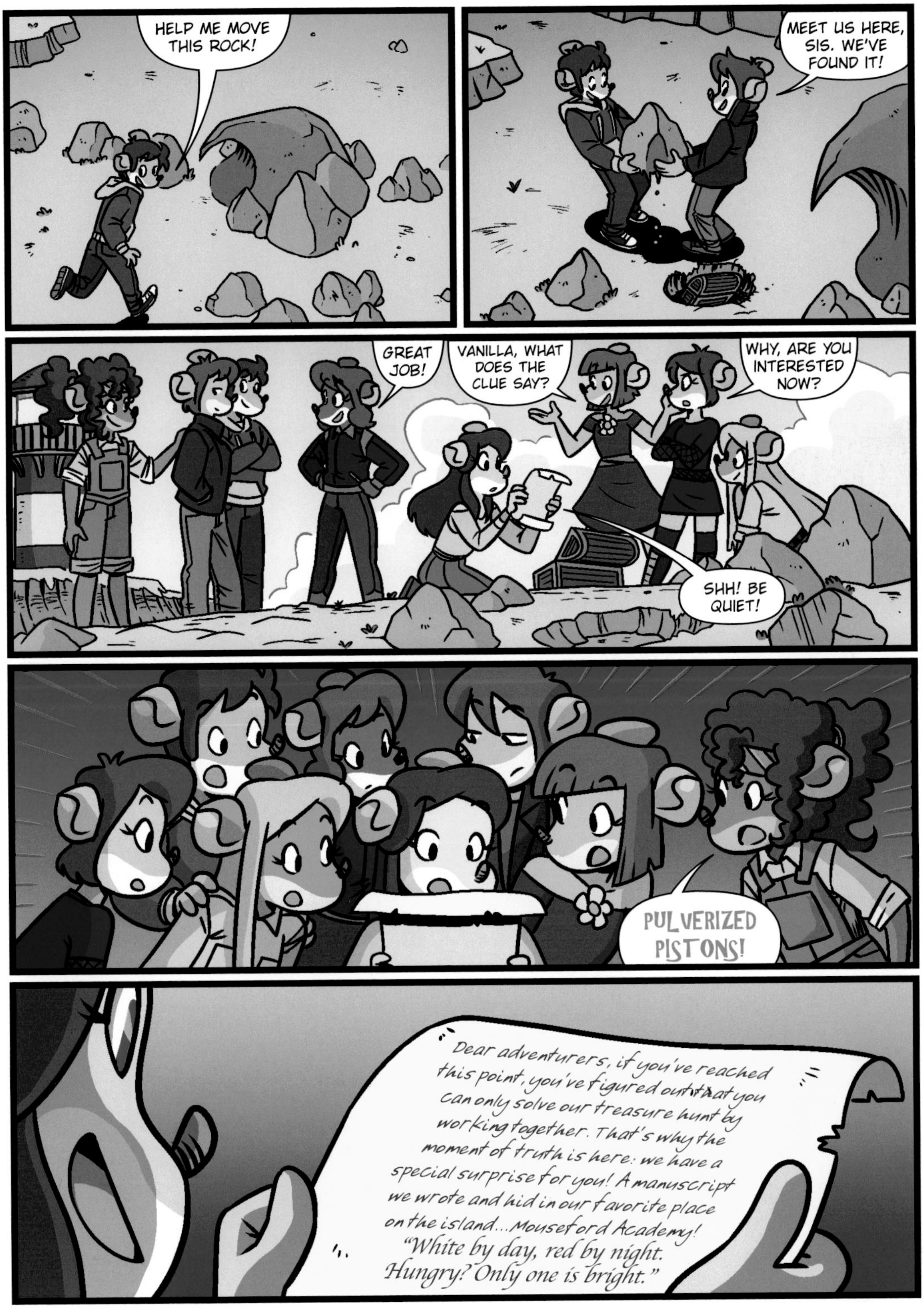
HELP ME MOVE THIS ROCK!
MEET US HERE, SIS. WE'VE FOUND IT!
GREAT JOB!
VANILLA, WHAT DOES THE CLUE SAY?
WHY, ARE YOU INTERESTED NOW?
SHH! BE QUIET!
PULVERIZED PISTONS!
Dear adventurers, if you've reached this point, you've figured out that you can only solve our treasure hunt by working together. That's why the moment of truth is here: we have a special surprise for you! A manuscript we wrote and hid in our favorite place on the island... Mouseford Academy!
"White by day, red by night. Hungry? Only one is bright."

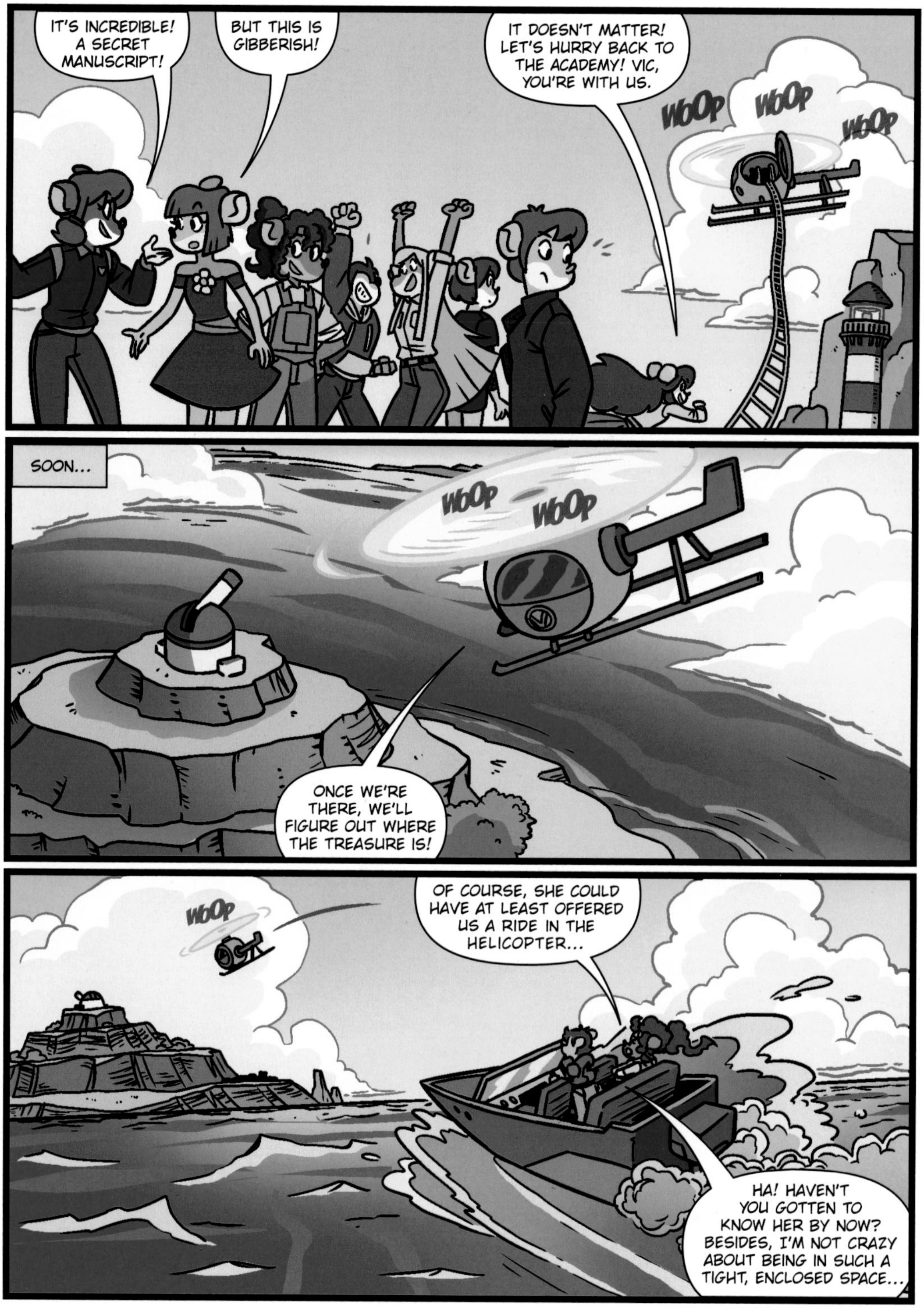
IT'S INCREDIBLE! A SECRET MANUSCRIPT!
BUT THIS IS GIBBERISH!
IT DOESN'T MATTER! LET'S HURRY BACK TO THE ACADEMY! VIC, YOU'RE WITH US.
WOOP WOOP WOOP
SOON...
WOOP WOOP
ONCE WE'RE THERE, WE'LL FIGURE OUT WHERE THE TREASURE IS!
WOOP
OF COURSE, SHE COULD HAVE AT LEAST OFFERED US A RIDE IN THE HELICOPTER...
HA! HAVEN'T YOU GOTTEN TO KNOW HER BY NOW? BESIDES, I'M NOT CRAZY ABOUT BEING IN SUCH A TIGHT, ENCLOSED SPACE...

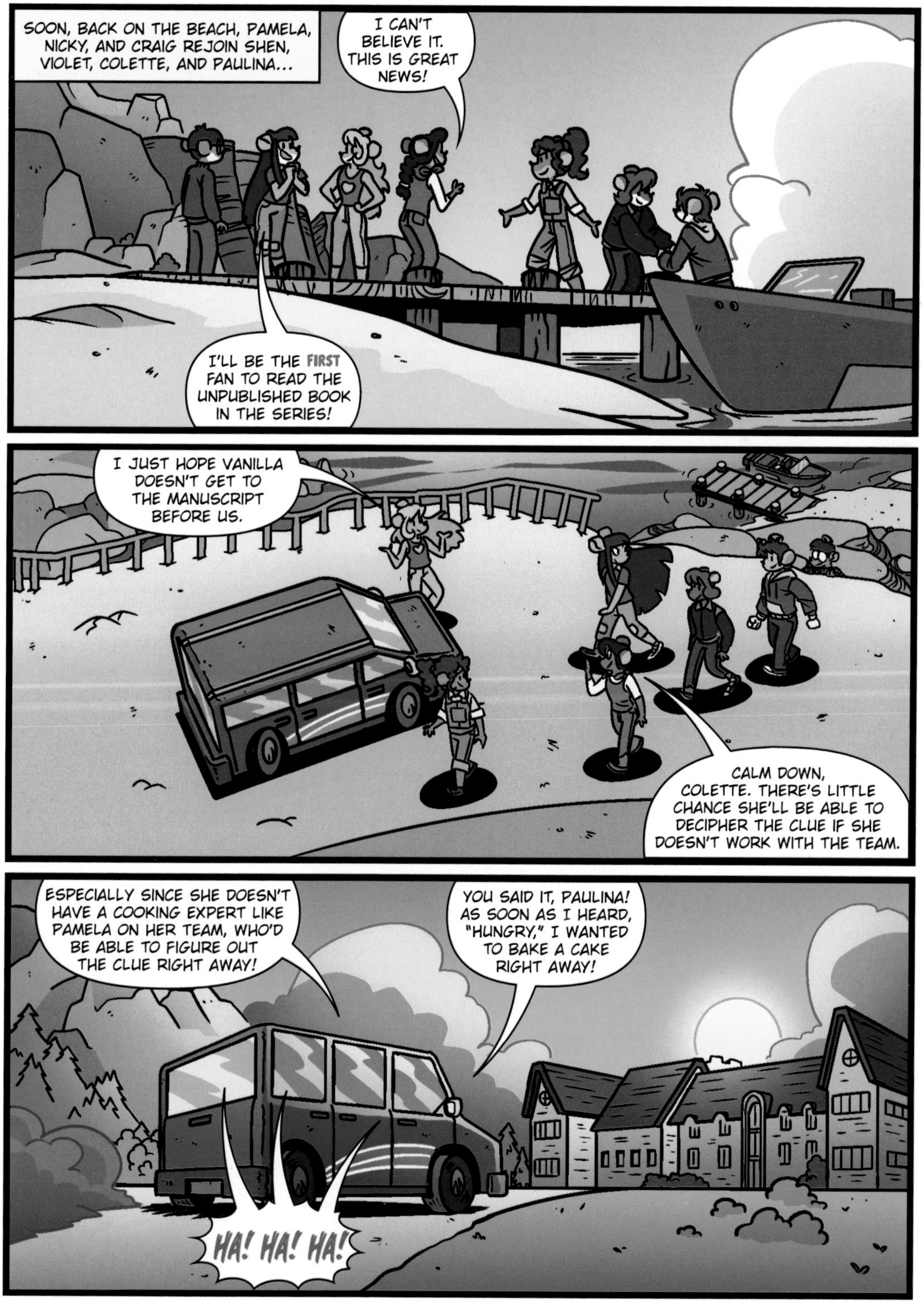
SOON, BACK ON THE BEACH, PAMELA, NICKY, AND CRAIG REJOIN SHEN, VIOLET, COLETTE, AND PAULINA...
I CAN'T BELIEVE IT. THIS IS GREAT NEWS!
I'LL BE THE FIRST FAN TO READ THE UNPUBLISHED BOOK IN THE SERIES!
I JUST HOPE VANILLA DOESN'T GET TO THE MANUSCRIPT BEFORE US.
CALM DOWN, COLETTE. THERE'S LITTLE CHANCE SHE'LL BE ABLE TO DECIPHER THE CLUE IF SHE DOESN'T WORK WITH THE TEAM.
ESPECIALLY SINCE SHE DOESN'T HAVE A COOKING EXPERT LIKE PAMELA ON HER TEAM, WHO'D BE ABLE TO FIGURE OUT THE CLUE RIGHT AWAY!
YOU SAID IT, PAULINA! AS SOON AS I HEARD, "HUNGRY," I WANTED TO BAKE A CAKE RIGHT AWAY!
HA! HA! HA!

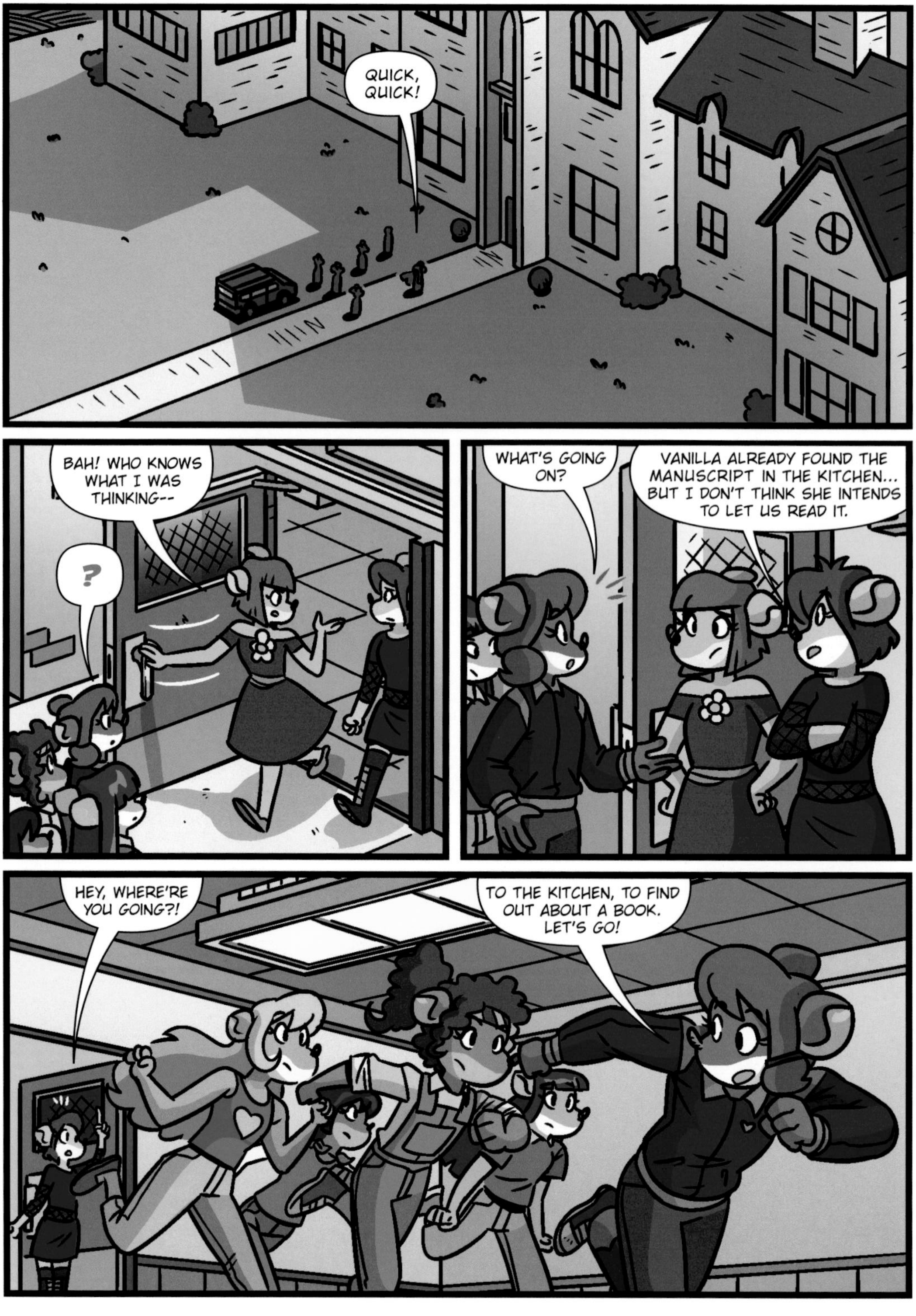
QUICK, QUICK!
BAH! WHO KNOWS WHAT I WAS THINKING--
?
WHAT'S GOING ON?
VANILLA ALREADY FOUND THE MANUSCRIPT IN THE KITCHEN... BUT I DON'T THINK SHE INTENDS TO LET US READ IT.
HEY, WHERE'RE YOU GOING?!
TO THE KITCHEN, TO FIND OUT ABOUT A BOOK. LET'S GO!

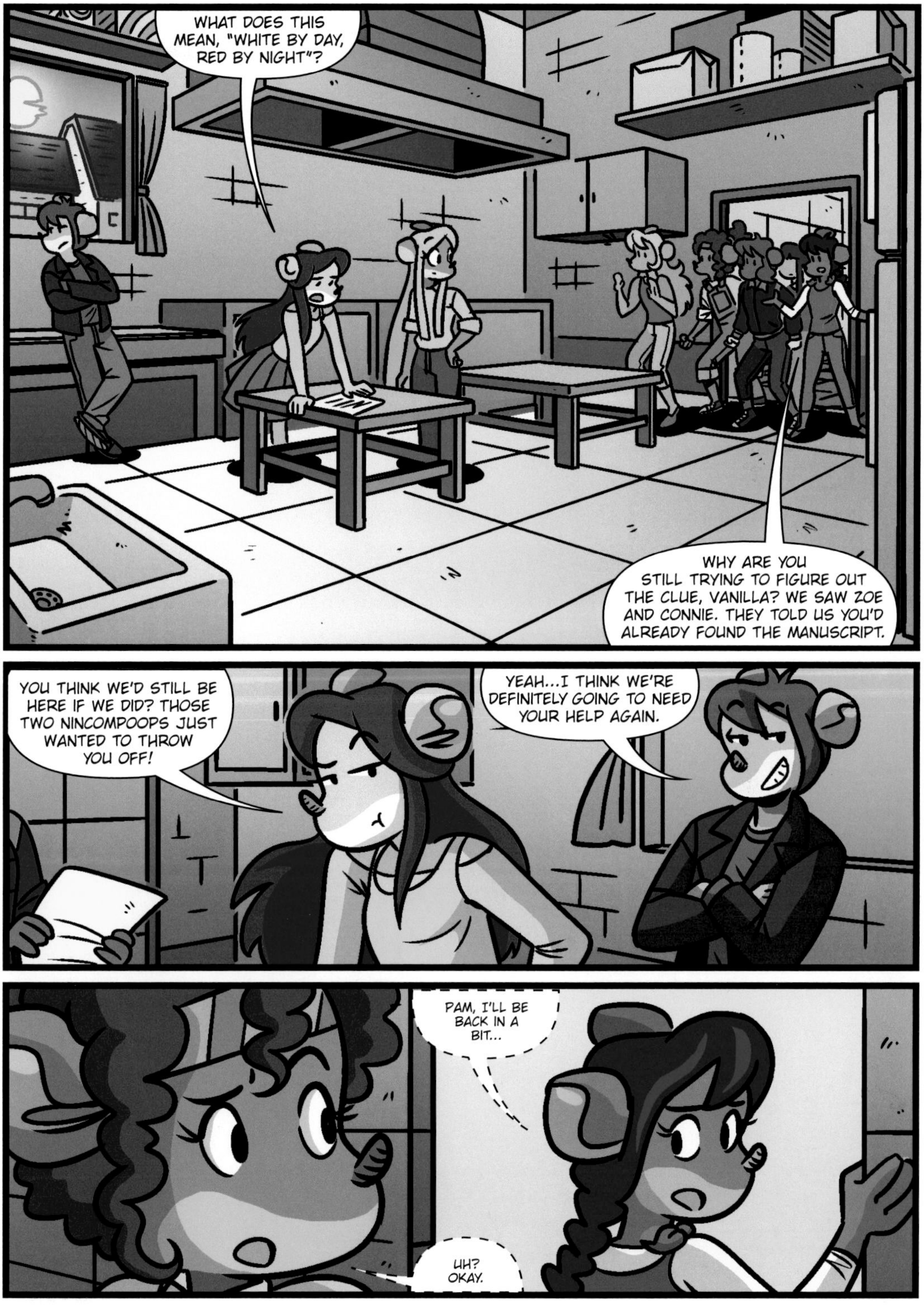
WHAT DOES THIS MEAN, "WHITE BY DAY, RED BY NIGHT"?
WHY ARE YOU STILL TRYING TO FIGURE OUT THE CLUE, VANILLA? WE SAW ZOE AND CONNIE. THEY TOLD US YOU'D ALREADY FOUND THE MANUSCRIPT.
YOU THINK WE'D STILL BE HERE IF WE DID? THOSE TWO NINCOMPOOPS JUST WANTED TO THROW YOU OFF!
YEAH...I THINK WE'RE DEFINITELY GOING TO NEED YOUR HELP AGAIN.
PAM, I'LL BE BACK IN A BIT...
UH? OKAY.

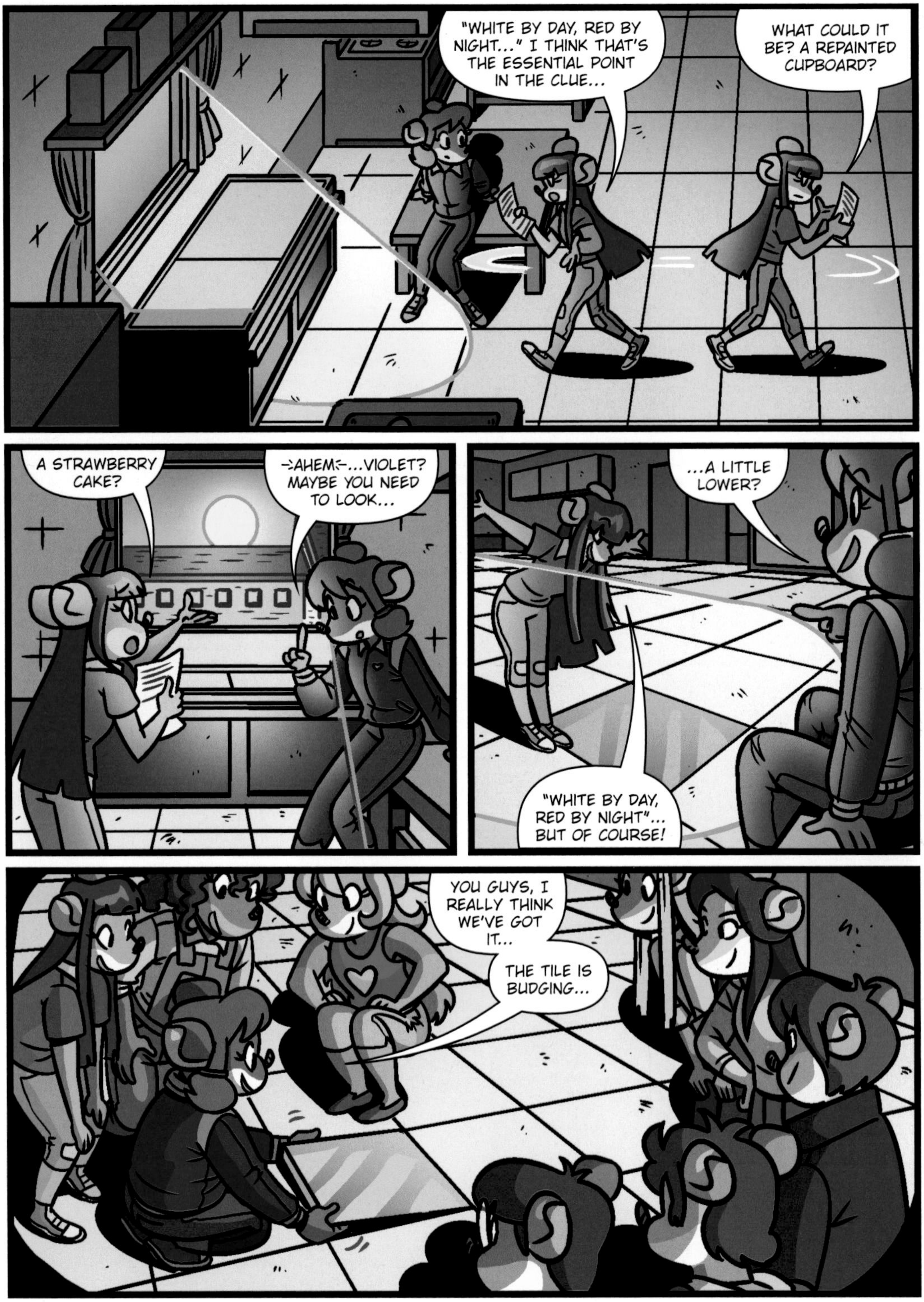
"WHITE BY DAY, RED BY NIGHT..." I THINK THAT'S THE ESSENTIAL POINT IN THE CLUE...
WHAT COULD IT BE? A REPAINTED CUPBOARD?
A STRAWBERRY CAKE?
AHEM...VIOLET? MAYBE YOU NEED TO LOOK...
...A LITTLE LOWER?
"WHITE BY DAY, RED BY NIGHT"... BUT OF COURSE!
YOU GUYS, I REALLY THINK WE'VE GOT IT...
THE TILE IS BUDGING...

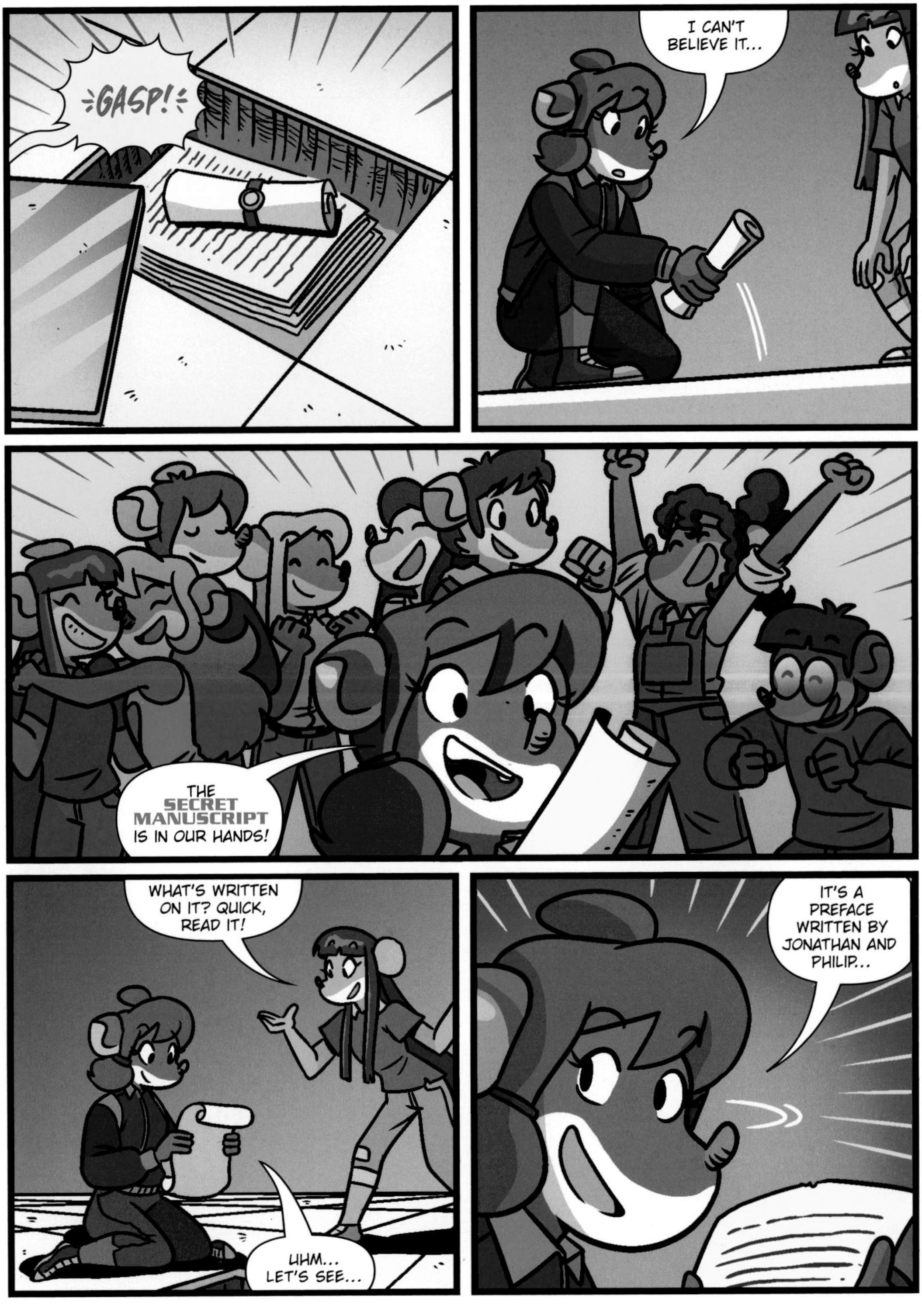
GASP!
I CAN'T BELIEVE IT...
THE SECRET MANUSCRIPT IS IN OUR HANDS!
WHAT'S WRITTEN ON IT? QUICK, READ IT!
UHM... LET'S SEE...
IT'S A PREFACE WRITTEN BY JONATHAN AND PHILIP...

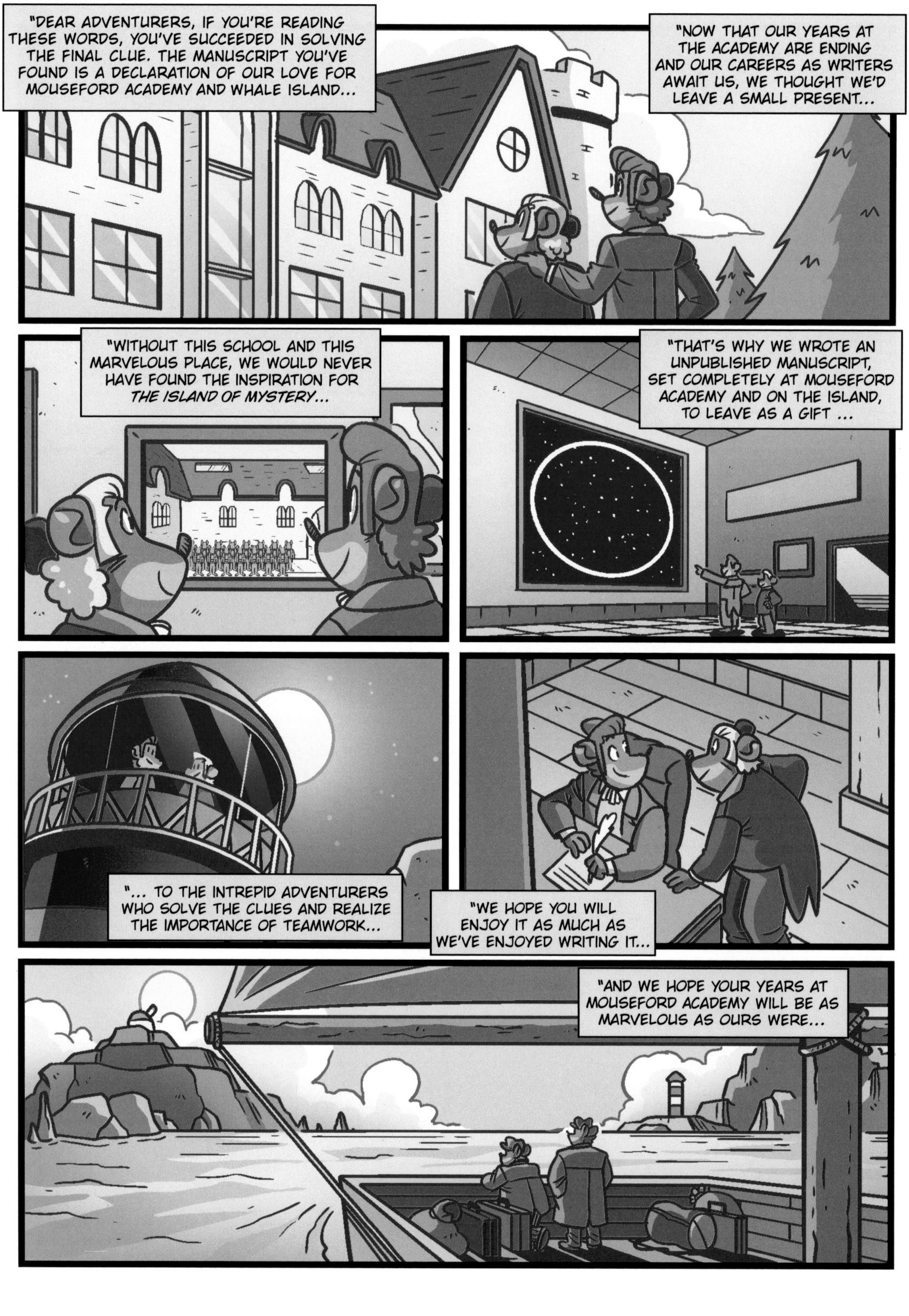
"DEAR ADVENTURERS, IF YOU'RE READING THESE WORDS, YOU'VE SUCCEEDED IN SOLVING THE FINAL CLUE. THE MANUSCRIPT YOU'VE FOUND IS A DECLARATION OF OUR LOVE FOR MOUSEFORD ACADEMY AND WHALE ISLAND...
"NOW THAT OUR YEARS AT THE ACADEMY ARE ENDING AND OUR CAREERS AS WRITERS AWAIT US, WE THOUGHT WE'D LEAVE A SMALL PRESENT...
"WITHOUT THIS SCHOOL AND THIS MARVELOUS PLACE, WE WOULD NEVER HAVE FOUND THE INSPIRATION FOR *THE ISLAND OF MYSTERY*...
"THAT'S WHY WE WROTE AN UNPUBLISHED MANUSCRIPT, SET COMPLETELY AT MOUSEFORD ACADEMY AND ON THE ISLAND, TO LEAVE AS A GIFT ...
"... TO THE INTREPID ADVENTURERS WHO SOLVE THE CLUES AND REALIZE THE IMPORTANCE OF TEAMWORK...
"WE HOPE YOU WILL ENJOY IT AS MUCH AS WE'VE ENJOYED WRITING IT...
"AND WE HOPE YOUR YEARS AT MOUSEFORD ACADEMY WILL BE AS MARVELOUS AS OURS WERE...

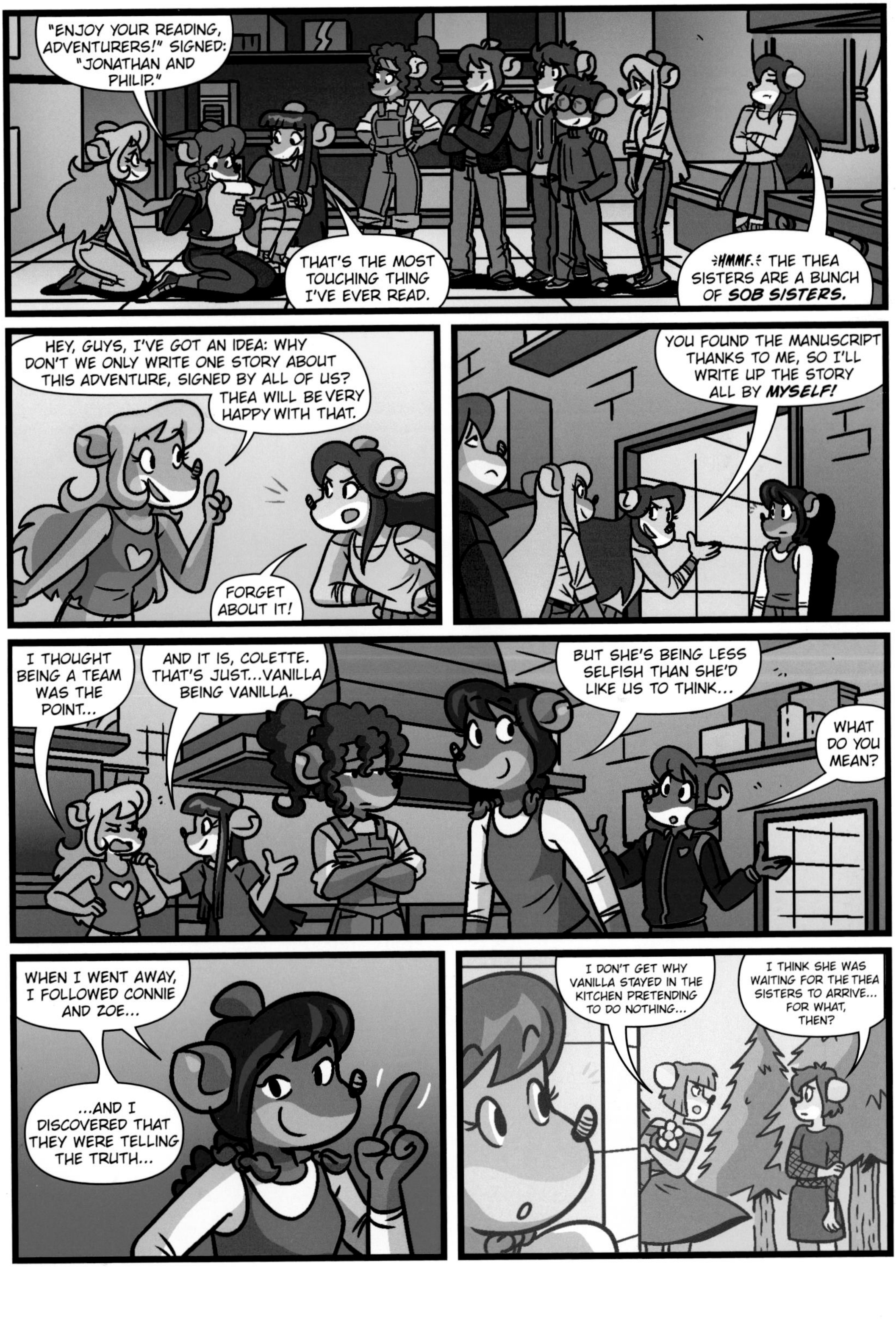
"ENJOY YOUR READING, ADVENTURERS!" SIGNED: "JONATHAN AND PHILIP."
THAT'S THE MOST TOUCHING THING I'VE EVER READ.
HMMF. THE THEA SISTERS ARE A BUNCH OF SOB SISTERS.
HEY, GUYS, I'VE GOT AN IDEA: WHY DON'T WE ONLY WRITE ONE STORY ABOUT THIS ADVENTURE, SIGNED BY ALL OF US? THEA WILL BE VERY HAPPY WITH THAT.
FORGET ABOUT IT!
YOU FOUND THE MANUSCRIPT THANKS TO ME, SO I'LL WRITE UP THE STORY ALL BY MYSELF!
I THOUGHT BEING A TEAM WAS THE POINT...
AND IT IS, COLETTE. THAT'S JUST...VANILLA BEING VANILLA.
BUT SHE'S BEING LESS SELFISH THAN SHE'D LIKE US TO THINK...
WHAT DO YOU MEAN?
WHEN I WENT AWAY, I FOLLOWED CONNIE AND ZOE...
...AND I DISCOVERED THAT THEY WERE TELLING THE TRUTH...
I DON'T GET WHY VANILLA STAYED IN THE KITCHEN PRETENDING TO DO NOTHING...
I THINK SHE WAS WAITING FOR THE THEA SISTERS TO ARRIVE... FOR WHAT, THEN?

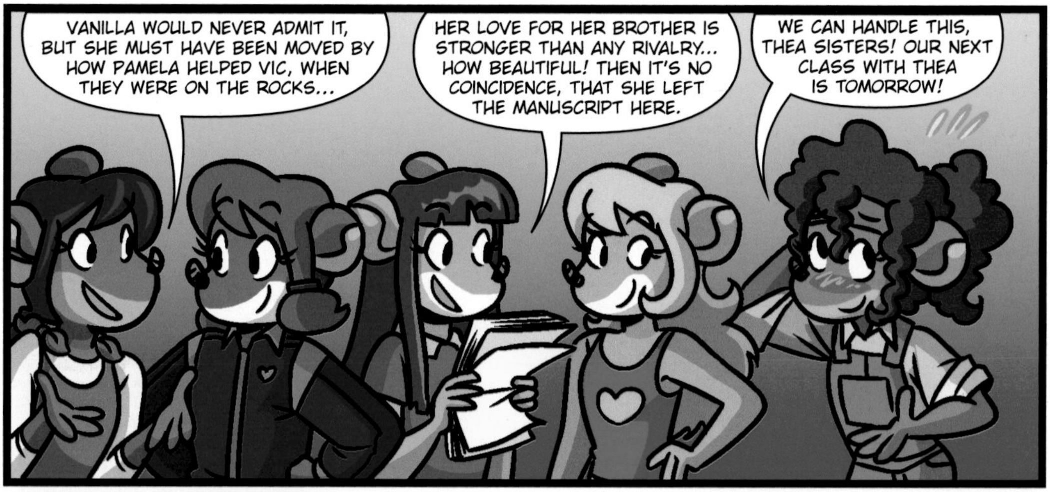
VANILLA WOULD NEVER ADMIT IT, BUT SHE MUST HAVE BEEN MOVED BY HOW PAMELA HELPED VIC, WHEN THEY WERE ON THE ROCKS...
HER LOVE FOR HER BROTHER IS STRONGER THAN ANY RIVALRY... HOW BEAUTIFUL! THEN IT'S NO COINCIDENCE, THAT SHE LEFT THE MANUSCRIPT HERE.
WE CAN HANDLE THIS, THEA SISTERS! OUR NEXT CLASS WITH THEA IS TOMORROW!

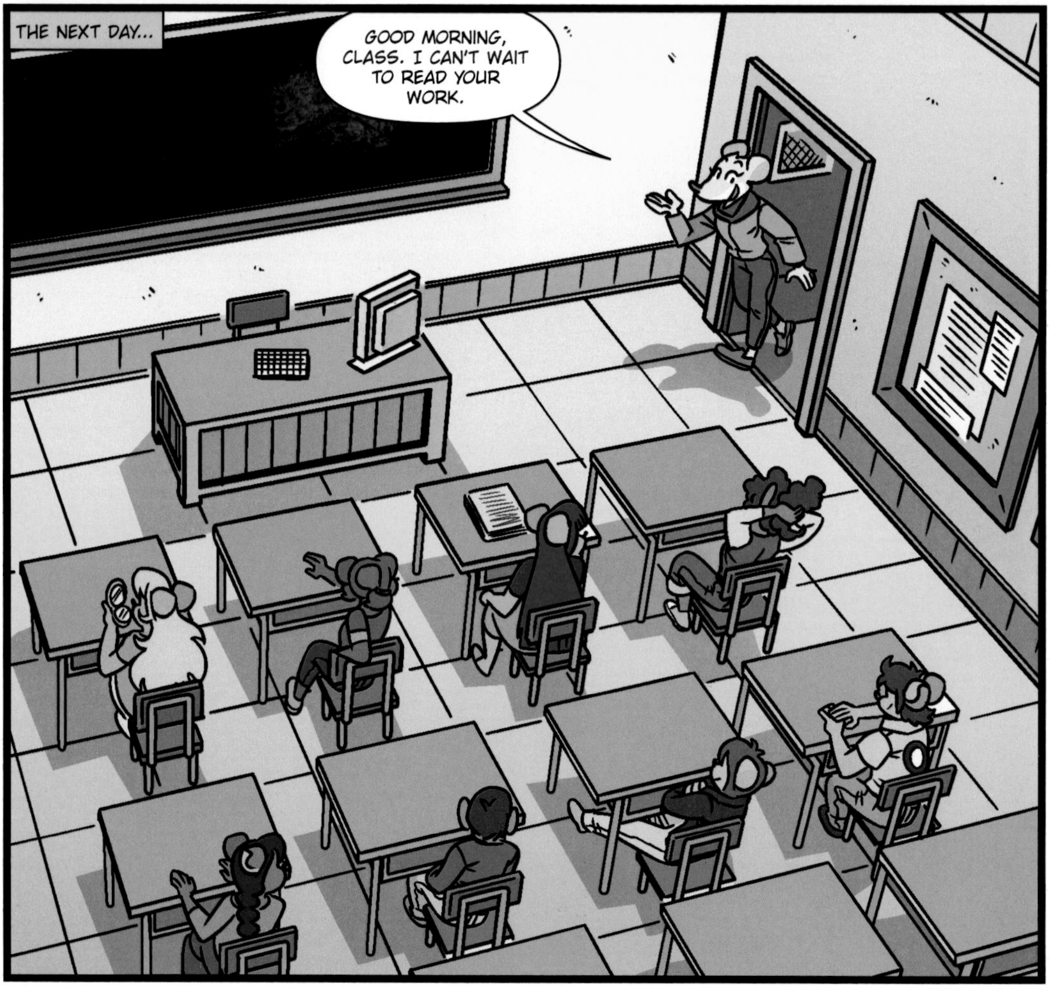
THE NEXT DAY...
GOOD MORNING, CLASS. I CAN'T WAIT TO READ YOUR WORK.

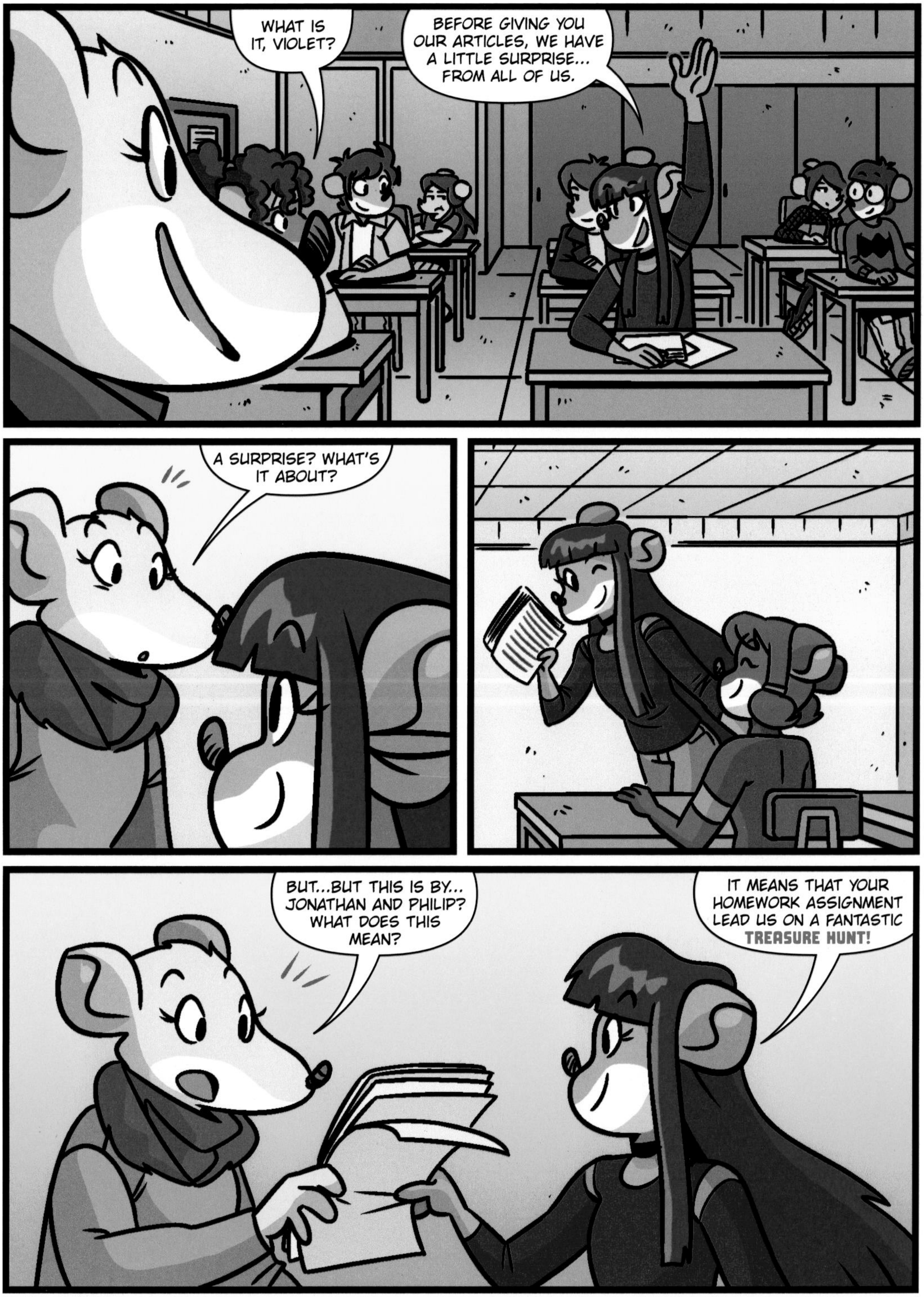
WHAT IS IT, VIOLET?
BEFORE GIVING YOU OUR ARTICLES, WE HAVE A LITTLE SURPRISE... FROM ALL OF US.
A SURPRISE? WHAT'S IT ABOUT?
BUT...BUT THIS IS BY... JONATHAN AND PHILIP? WHAT DOES THIS MEAN?
IT MEANS THAT YOUR HOMEWORK ASSIGNMENT LEAD US ON A FANTASTIC TREASURE HUNT!

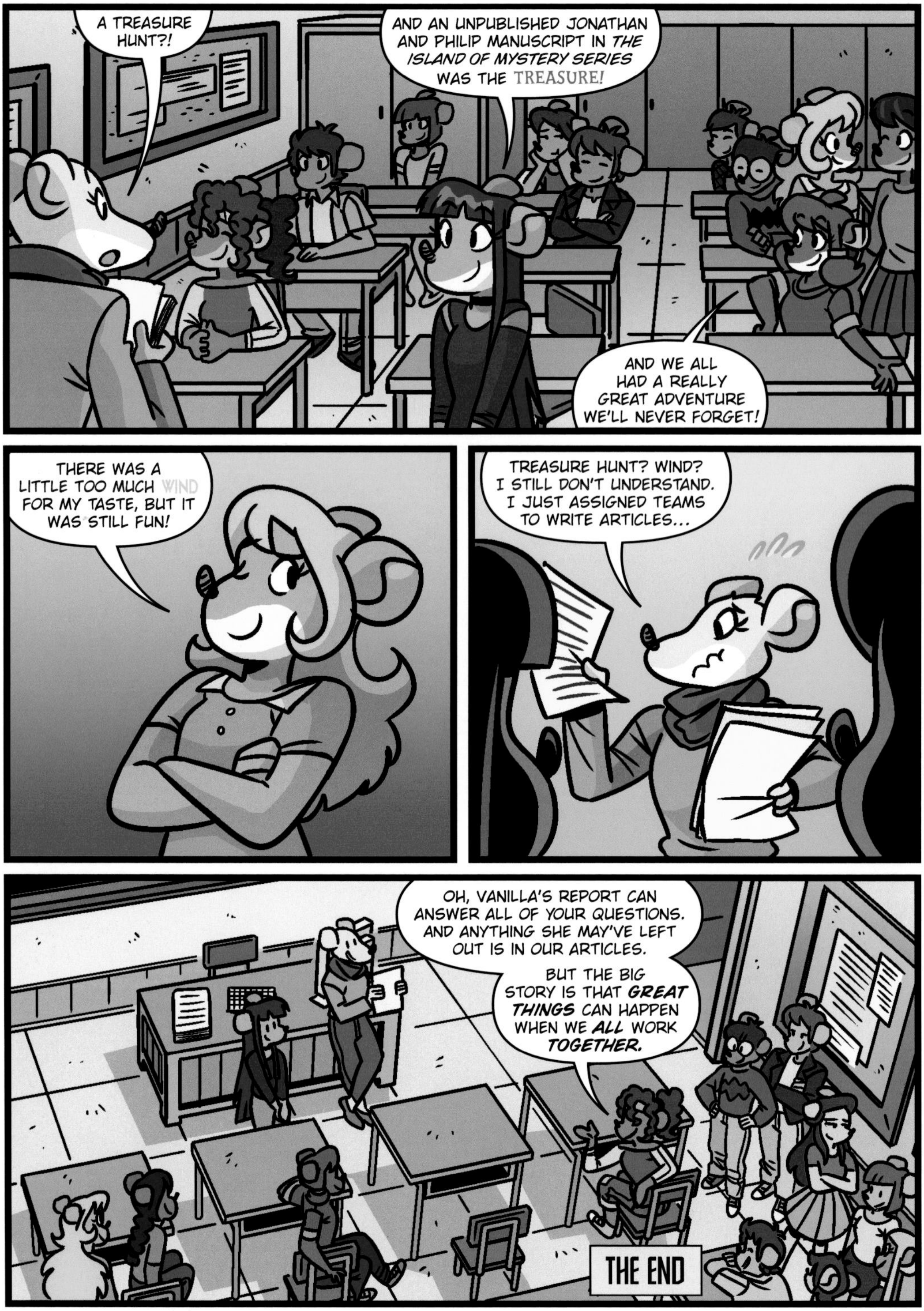
A TREASURE HUNT?!
AND AN UNPUBLISHED JONATHAN AND PHILIP MANUSCRIPT IN *THE ISLAND OF MYSTERY SERIES* WAS THE TREASURE!
AND WE ALL HAD A REALLY GREAT ADVENTURE WE'LL NEVER FORGET!
THERE WAS A LITTLE TOO MUCH WIND FOR MY TASTE, BUT IT WAS STILL FUN!
TREASURE HUNT? WIND? I STILL DON'T UNDERSTAND. I JUST ASSIGNED TEAMS TO WRITE ARTICLES...
OH, VANILLA'S REPORT CAN ANSWER ALL OF YOUR QUESTIONS. AND ANYTHING SHE MAY'VE LEFT OUT IS IN OUR ARTICLES.
BUT THE BIG STORY IS THAT **GREAT THINGS** CAN HAPPEN WHEN WE **ALL** WORK **TOGETHER.**
THE END

Watch Out For PAPERCUTZ™

Welcome to the excessively-windy, enchantingly-enlightening, eighth THEA STILTON graphic novel reported by Thea Stilton (as told to Francesco Savino, writer, and Ryan Jampole, artist) from Papercutz, that scholarly bunch dedicated to publishing great graphic novels for all ages. I'm Salicrup, *Jim Salicrup* the Editor-in-Chief and chief windbag, here to report some actual news…

FAKE NEWS ALERT: Wilson Ramos Jr. can't really play guitar, but he can play *RockBand*!

Francesco Savino does play guitar!

First, to follow up on a minor story we first reported on in THEA STILTON #7, in which we saw how musically talented the Thea Sisters happen to be, we also noted that Papercutz publisher Terry Nantier could play the drums, and our erstwhile Production Coordinator, Sasha Kimiatek, plays violin. We promised to see if any other members of our creative crew played any musical instruments and to report our findings here. We did a lot of research and extensive digging (actually we just sent out a few emails) and discovered that writer Francesco Savino actually plays guitar, artist Ryan Jampole plays guitar, that colorist Laurie E. Smith doesn't play a musical instrument, but she does voiceovers, letterer Wilson Ramos Jr. plays guitar—well, if you count the one in the game *RockBand*–and translator Nanette McGuinness is a soprano (No, she's not a New Jersey mobster, she's also a professional opera singer). Or so they claim. A good journalist will get confirmation, we'll just have to take 'em on their word.

But the big news is actually about the fate of this particular series of graphic novels. As much as we love producing THEA STILTON graphic novels, due to circumstances beyond our control, we won't be publishing any further volumes in this series. Usually, when a publisher stops creating additional volumes in a series that means that the sales have fallen to the point where it doesn't make sense to continue, but let me assure you, THEA STILTON has been a wonderfully solid seller for us and we really wish we could continue, but as it's been said, all things must end, and for us this issue marks the end of our series of all-new THEA STILTON graphic novels featuring the Thea Sisters.

The good news is we're actually starting a new series, called THEA STILTON 3 IN 1, which will feature three THEA STILTON graphic novels in each volume. The first volume will re-present THEA STILTON #1-3, in an affordable paperback edition. If you missed those early THEA graphic novels, here's a great way to catch up.

We have even more exciting news! Yes, we've saved the best for last! Coming soon from Papercutz will be an all-new graphic novel series called MELOWY! It stars five female winged unicorns named Electra, Selene, Kora, Maia, and Clio, and it's all about their magical adventures at school at Destino, a legendary castle hidden somewhere in the clouds above the ancient realms of the world of Aura. If that wasn't awesome enough, each of these students was born with a symbol on their wings, a sign that they have a hidden power. We hope that you'll check out the first MELOWY graphic novel, and get to know these five girls—we suspect you may love them as much as you do The Thea Sisters!

So, as we sadly say good-bye to Whale Island and those five Mouseford Academy students, let's all say hello to the five new students at Destino—coming your way in MELOWY #1! Be sure to go to papercutz.com for more MELOWY news!

Meet the stars of MELOWY!

Thanks,

Jim

Stay in Touch!

Email: Papercutz@papercutz.com
Web: www.papercutz.com
Twitter: @papercutzgn
Instagram: @papercutzgn
Facebook: PAPERCUTZGRAPHICNOVELS
Snailmail: Papercutz, 160 Broadway, Suite 700,
            East Wing, New York, NY 10038

Vanilla de Vissen
is the daughter of the queen of cosmetics, Vissia de Vissen. Spoiled and capricious, she's very jealous of the Thea Sisters!

Zoe, Connie, and Alicia
are Vanilla's friends who will follow her every move and aid in every scheme.

Craig
is a Mouseford student, very good at sports but not so good at his studies! He and his friend Shen have a lot of fun together.